Mike's Dilemma

Mike's Dilemma
by Jannette Morrow

Copyright © 2006 Jannette Morrow
First Printing January 2007
Library of Congress Number pending

ISBN# 0-9791154-2-6
        978-0-9791154-2-4

Published by Main Street Publishing, Inc.,
Cover Design by Nia Bey and Shari B Hill
Illustrations by Nia Bey
Copy Editing by Shari B Hill
Editing by Pat Little
Printed and bound by NetPub, Poughkeepsie, NY.

For more information write Main Street Publishing, Inc.,
206 East Main St., Suite 207, P.O. Box 696, Jackson, TN 38302
Phone 1-731-427-7379 or toll free 1-866-457-7379.
E-mail:words@mspbooks.com for managing editor and
mspsupport@charterinternet.com for customer service. Visit us at
www.mainstreetpublishing.com and www.mspbooks.com.

Mike's Dilemma

by Jannette Morrow

Main Street Publishing, Inc., Jackson, TN

Table of Contents

In Memory of:
Audrey A. Morrow

Jannette Morrow

Prologue

Mike's Dilemma

SWOOSH! Shamael sheathed his sword and looked on thoughtfully as his enemy for the moment scurried away. "Score one more point for the forces of good over evil," he said to himself with a smile. But he didn't contemplate long over his victory; there would always be another fight just around the next corner to be sure. Besides, he had more important things to think about. Shamael knew that he was in for a new assignment. It had been many, many years (as humans reckon time) since he had taken on such an important task.

"He calls us. We'll be together on this one, you know," said Shamael's friend Jediael, who was just coming toward him. Like Shamael, Jediael was also a mighty guardian angel - tall, with shining face, fiery eyes, flowing robes tied with a brightly glowing golden belt, two giant wings that absolutely sparkled, and a huge sword ever at his side. Jediael had smooth dark sculpted features under a crown of dark wool like hair, and his eyes shone a bright emerald green. Shamael's face, however, was a ruddy, and his hair was shiny, straight, and blacker than a raven's wing. His fiery deep set eyes glittered dark blue like two huge sapphires.

"I know," replied Shamael, smiling back. And I hear Hanniel will be with us too.

"Hanniel?" said Jediael, raising his eyebrows. "Do you think he'll stay serious long enough to do this? I mean, assignments like this are always of the utmost importance to the Holy One, but this time..."

"Is especially important - I know," said Shamael. He reached out and patted his friend on the shoulder. "If the Holy One picked him, then he too must be the best one for the job. Let's go."

Traveling at the speed of thought, the pair soon came upon the two other angels that were waiting for them. Magdiel, their immediate superior, was majestic as always. He had flowing dark hair and stood head and shoulders taller than the others. He looked down on them serenely with crystal clear eyes that sparkled like diamonds. Next to him was Hanniel with his arms folded inside the long sleeves of his robe. His face shone with the color of a polished pearl, and a long gold braid hung down his back. Only his slight grin and his bright aquamarine eyes hinted at the mirth hidden beneath his otherwise austere appearance. The angels waited for their superior to speak first.

"I called the three of you here today because your new task will be bringing you together a great deal," Magdiel began. "This is especially for you, Shamael, as Jediael's charge was born three months ago, and it will be almost another two years, as humans reckon time, until Hanniel's charge comes into the world." Magdiel turned, and suddenly the four of them were standing unseen just above a bustling delivery room of a hospital in a small town called Chesterton. Just then, a doctor was showing a squalling newborn baby boy to an exhausted but happy mother, while a beaming father looked on.

"He's precious," said Shamael, "but so are all human babies. Why is this one...?"

"Because to whom much is given," said Magdiel quietly, "much is required."

"So what has he been given, besides a rather strong pair of lungs?" asked Hanniel.

"A great deal, Magdiel replied. His gifts will be made manifest - in time. But the enemy of men's souls will strongly desire to keep this one from fulfilling the Holy One's plan for him. Guard him well!" With that, Magdiel disappeared.

Mike's Dilemma

Chapter 1

Mike's Dilemma

Ordinary. O-r-d-i-n-a-r-y. The hands on the clock were moving at a snail's pace toward two forty-five while rain beat on the windows outside the classroom. Mike Bryant labored to fill in the word on his exam sheet. "When you hear the word, spell it correctly on your paper," Mrs. Hannaby said in her shrill voice. "Note whether it is a verb, noun, or adjective. Use it in a sentence..." Mike glanced out the window and thought of how the word described his eleven and a half year life. Ordinary. Mike gazed a moment at his face in the window's reflection hoping to see a face that was pop star handsome. He was disappointed as usual. Like his life, his face could only be described as ordinary at best. Close cut curly black hair, brown eyes, and brown face, his favorite blue and gray checkered shirt that he wore every chance he could get. Mike wrinkled his forehead, knitting his bushy eyebrows together. "Man-sized eyebrows," are what his dad, Mike, Sr. called them. "You'll have to grow into those," he said. He remembered Corrie Thompson telling him that most of the girls in the class thought he might be "sort of cute" if it weren't for his eyebrows. He managed to get elected class vice- president though, after Sunnie Powers who got the most votes, but she was the most popular kid in class.

Now it was the end of May, and not only would his term end but so would his years at Chesterton Elementary School. Mike and the rest of his class would be graduating this year and going off to Chesterton Central

Junior High, and he found the thought of it to be a bit scary, even as he wrote his ordinary sentence on this ordinary day in his ordinary life. Mike briefly wondered if stuff like this ever bothered his best friend, Joey Edwards. Joey never seemed to worry about anything but his next antic or practical joke. And, of course, no one would have elected Joey for anything - except maybe class clown. Mike turned back to his paper, wondering if he would ever be handsome or even noticeable and if anything really exiting would ever happen to him. Twenty minutes later Mike and Joey were under Mike's dad's big umbrella and dodging puddles as they walked home. Mike let Joey hold it since Joey was a bit taller.

"You want to go *where*?" asked Mike incredulously.

"The old Palmer house," insisted Joey, his hazel eyes widening in his tan face under a shock of never-combed reddish-brown hair. "It's Memorial Day this weekend so nobody'll be there - they *always* go away on holiday weekends."

"How do you know?"

"My stepbrother Danny told me. His grandma used to work for old Mr. Palmer , and she is still friends with them."

"So what's so great about that old house?" asked Mike.

"They've got all this really cool junk in the basement from the olden days *and* there's a ghost- maybe ghosts!"

"Ghosts?" Mike asked, his eyes wide too. "So how are we supposed to get in?"

"Through the back," answered Joey. "There's an old entrance right into the basement from the backyard."

"Won't it be locked?"

"Danny says he heard his grandma say that she was worried because the lock on the basement doors was broken, but old man Palmer never fixed it."

"Is Danny coming with us?" asked Mike. "And it'll have to be after choir practice. Mom never lets me out of that." Suddenly, both boys heard a huge 'SPLISH'. They jumped just in time to avoid most of the muddy water shooting out from under the wheels of a huge black SUV as it sped around the corner, splashing thick dirty liquid in every direction. The vehicle slowed and the window opened.

"Hey, it's 'Gorilla Face' and the 'Zebra.' Did we getcha? Too Baaad!" Rick Jefferies' sneering face disappeared as the window rolled up and the SUV sped off.

"Gosh, I hate him," muttered Mike, almost under his breath, remembering his mom's lecture to him about never hating anyone. Not even squinty eyed, brawny Rick, who lived on their block and was best known for getting kicked off Central High's football team for bad grades and bullying younger kids.

Joey shrugged. "He's a jerk; forget him. Anyway, I don't know yet if Danny is coming. It's his and Teddy's weekend to come over, but you know how Danny can be such a scaredy cat sometimes. Their mom, Ms.

Ellen, hardly ever lets them go anyplace."

* * * * * *

For the whole time that the boys talked about their plan - calling Danny, keeping his pesky kid brother Teddy out of the way, and where to meet. Shamael and Jediael silently watched from above, completely invisible to them. Shamael shook his head, thinking of all the thousands of boys he guarded over thousands of years and the thousands of times they got themselves into trouble. Of all the silly and possibly dangerous things to go after - ghosts!

"Do you think they'll go through with this cockamamie plan?" Jediael asked.

"How long have you known humans?" replied Shamael. "Do you think they won't?"

Jediael smiled in agreement.

* * * * * *

Meanwhile, Awmal sat pouting in a dark corner in what could have been a million miles away. He was remembering how once, very long ago, he was as noble as Shamael, Jediael, and countless others, but he wasn't anything like them now - not anymore. Now his world was totally different, and he was at the bottom. Princes, powers, rulers… all of them ranked higher than he did. The more he thought about it the more his pout slowly turned into a scowl, which wasn't much different than the rest of his green face. Wide floppy ears, a snout, which was turned up like a pig's, spindly arms and legs, and a scowl. It wasn't always this way. Awmal's mind drifted back to millennia on top of millennia ago when they were all beautiful - beautiful singing, beautiful wings, flying back and forth worshiping the Holy One. But now, thinking about the Holy One always brought him feelings of terror and despair, so now he forced back his original thought. If he were a prince or a ruler, he would be more significant. As it was, he only had a bit of authority to act, and then only with permission. But even their Supreme Ruler, Lucifer, needed permission. Almost before he realized it, Awmal snapped himself to attention. His immediate superior Nawgaf just invaded his space and his thoughts. Nawgaf was bigger, stronger, and even uglier than Awmal himself who thought his boss looked like a gorilla melded with a crocodile. Nawgaf overwhelmed him and everyone else less powerful than himself.

"I have an assignment for you," Nawgaf growled.

"What now, my superior?"

"It seems a certain young boy is going ghost hunting."

"So?" Being weaker didn't mean he had to be polite.

"So," said Nawgaf with mock patience. "I want him to find what he's looking for - AND I WANT YOU TO MAKE SURE THAT HE DOES!!"

Awmal would have yelled back, but the prospect of pain stopped him, so he carefully lowered his voice. "Superior, why am I given such insignificant tasks? Millennia after millennia I am assigned to the minuscule: reptiles, Ouija boards, séances. Have I not been diligent? Have I not performed well? Must I now pretend to be a ghost for these...these (he spat out the word) *children?* I know that I am the most humble and base of our race, but..."

"Spare me. Yes, you have done well. And this one may be a child, but he's..." Nawgaf paused. "Important."

"Really?"

"Yes - to that *other* cause. Or he will be if he can get that far. I'm counting on you to see that he doesn't. Get it?"

"Got it."

"Good. Dismissed."

Chapter 2

Mike's Dilemma

The Saturday morning sun shone through the windows on the floor and pews in stained glass multi-colors as choir practice began. Twenty three angels stood like an unseen honor guard around the walls of Community Fellowship Church, looking down with approval on the twenty-three noisy kids who were bustling around to find seats in their respective sections. Sopranos stood on the right and altos were on the left. And, as always, the boys were in the middle where Mrs. Roberts, the pastor's wife and Youth Choir director, could keep a better eye on them. Choir practice had barely started, but Mike was shuffling his feet, rolling his eyes, and wishing it was over.

"Tenors stand!" Mike went through his paces with the rest of the boys and one or two girls who were singing tenor. Just when it seemed like they would never stop singing the last chorus, Mrs. Roberts ended the song and asked everyone to sit down. Then she stepped out the side door to the hall to wave someone in.

"Children," she said in her sonorous voice, "this is our visiting minister for the summer. He will be helping us with our Summer Youth program and Vacation Bible School this year. His name is Reverend David Palmer."

When choir practice was finally over, Mike raced out of the church and started looking for a flashlight as soon as he got into the house.

"So, why do you need a flashlight?" Meg Bryant demanded in her crisp Jamaican accent.

"Mom! I just want to take it with us. "

"Don't evade me, boy. Where are you going that's so dark that you need a flashlight in broad daylight?" As usual, his mom didn't miss a thing. Mike sighed, put the flashlight back, and slid out the door and across the street. Joey, Danny, Teddy, and their dad Mr. Greg Edwards were just on their way to McDonald's. Mike didn't have to be invited twice and climbed into the minivan once his mom looked out the door and waved her permission.

"Will you get off me? Dad, Teddy's bothering me, and he won't stay in his seat!" Joey shouted from the back while Mike was settling in.

"I know what seat I'm going to be on if I have to stop this car," replied their dad, "and I don't mean the one bolted to the floor!" That kept the boys quiet for a few minutes until Mike was safely buckled in between his two friends. As soon they were on the road. Teddy began to bug their dad about a Happy Meal and toy. Joey took the opportunity to lean towards Danny.

"Me and Mike- we're going to the old Palmer house to find the ghost. Wanna come?"

"What?" said Danny.

"Do you want to come with us to find the ghost?" Mike whispered just loud enough to be heard over the engine, the radio, and Teddy's chattering.

"What are you boys whispering about back there?" asked Mr. Edwards.

"We said we want the cola and fries the most, Dad," called back Joey.

Mr. Edwards said he wasn't too sure about that, but by then they had arrived at the restaurant. Inside, the seats were too close together to say more, so Joey nudged Mike and told Danny "We'll tell you later."

* * * * * *

When later came, (two hours later to be exact) Shamael, Hanniel, and Jediael stood silently against the back wall of the basement in the Palmer house. Glancing across the room, they could see that Awmal was ready and waiting, sitting with his head between his drawn-up knobby knees. Hanniel sent a thought to Shamael.

"I'm sure he knows we're around here someplace."

"Yes," returned Shamael, just as silently, "but he's too consumed with his plan to bother about us - yet. After all, they'll be here any moment now."

* * * * * *

The old flat metal doors made a loud creaking noise when Mike and Joey started to pull them open, sending a stream of sunlight into the dark basement. The underground steps and the doors that lead to them were surrounded by a fence and a gate with a rusty lock but that didn't stop the boys from scrambling over it. Most importantly, just as Danny's grandma had said, the doors themselves had no lock.

"You go first!" said Mike.

"I'm not going first - *you* go!" replied Joey.

"You have the flashlight."

"Alright already - I'll go," said Joey who managed to get a flashlight from his step dad's toolbox without anyone noticing.

"And are you guys sure that Teddy didn't try to follow you?" asked Mike.

"I'm sure," replied Joey. "I said he could play with my new Game Boy - he'll be busy for hours." He turned to face Danny. "Are you coming or not?"

"I don't think I like this, you guys," answered Danny, who was standing with his thin shoulders pressed against the brick wall of the house. He was almost as brown as the old bricks, and his huge dark eyes looked smaller because of his thick eyeglasses. He had just turned ten years old, but he was only as tall as Joey's shoulders. Danny peered down the basement steps. "My mom would go ballistic if she knew I was here!"

The old Palmer place was just that - old. It was more of a mansion than just a house, and it had been there as long as anyone in the town could remember. Old timers said that it was the Big House, when most of what was now their neighborhood was still farmland. Not that the property was so terribly small now. The house sat on an acre and a half of land that had gradually grown into a small forest. Despite its stately appearance from a distance, closer inspection of the house revealed several broken windows, a roof badly in need of repair, places where the bricks had fallen out, and gardens that had long since gone back to nature. Since rumors already surrounded the place like moths surround a flame, the recent presence of workmen going in and out of the house caused the gossip to spread all the more. People talked about murder, mobsters, even a stash of money buried in the basement from a bank robbery many years ago. No one lived there anymore except Old Mr. Palmer, who was about the fourth or fifth Mr. Palmer to be born there, and his wife. Both were getting on in years and were a bit forgetful. Everyone in the neighborhood expected that the Palmers' grown children would move out the old couple and sell the old wreck of a house. "It only makes sense," Joey's mom had said to Mike's mom a few days ago. "Why else would they go to visit their children nearly every week if they weren't planning to move in with them?"

"Come on, Danny. Don't be a chicken," said Mike teasingly. "You came this far, so you may as well come in too. Nobody but us will know."

* * * * * *

"Famous last words," murmured Shamael to the two angels that were with him as they looked up from the basement through the wall at the three boys hesitating in the yard. "I wonder if Mike realizes the connection between the Pastor David Palmer that he saw in choir practice and the name, Old Palmer House." Danny's angel Hanniel was smiling in spite of the situation.

"He's such a wonderful boy."

"Who?" said Jediael.

"Why, my Danny, of course."

Shamael and Jediael exchanged knowing glances. Every millennia Hanniel always had "such wonderful" boys and girls.

"What's so wonderful about him?" said Jediael with a wink at Shamael. Isn't he here too?"

"Yes, but he doesn't want to be," answered Hanniel confidently. "He'll be the first one to do the right thing, just you wait and see."

Shamael smiled at that, but he was still worried, and not just about the three boys who were now carefully picking their way down the basement steps behind the thin beam of the flashlight. He was also concerned about the two malevolent red eyes now looking up at him from the corner, as invisible to Mike, Danny, and Joey as the angels themselves were.

Shamael silently drew his sword, as did the other two angels, before addressing Awmal.

"What do you want?"

"What do you think?"

"There's no reason for you to interfere," said Shamael.

"But as you yourselves said, they're here," retorted Awmal. "And you and I both know what they intend to do. I'm within my rights!"

Shamael didn't bother to respond but turned his attention back to Mike and the other boys. Awmal would certainly have been no threat to him, even if he were alone. What he didn't like was the unfortunate fact that he couldn't even say "The Lord rebuke you" to Awmal on this one.

"His rights!" said Jediael indignantly. "He has the gall to talk about 'his rights'!"

"He has a point though," replied Shamael. "They are here without permission, and if they really try to scare up a ghost..." Joey's voice interrupted.

"Wow! Guys look at this!" By now, the boys had ventured further into the basement and had come upon some old objects. There was furniture, several old trunks, and the object of Joey's attention: an old suit of armor that was standing right in the middle of the floor. The thing was downright eerie looking in the dim light and moving shadows. Flecks of sunlight filtered through the dirt covered window at the far end of the room. Cobwebs dangled from the ceiling.

"This place is creepy, and I never smelled anything so musty in my whole life," said Danny between coughs. "And I think I hear footsteps. Guys, we need to get out of here."

"Will you be quiet?" said Mike in a loud whisper.

"Why?" said Joey in his regular voice. "Nobody but us is here."

"But I heard footsteps," insisted Danny. "What if there really *is* a ghost?"

"What's that in the doorway?" said Joey, aiming the flashlight at the far wall. "Let's go see!"

They had to step high over all the junk scattered on the floor around the old armor. They could barely squeeze past without brushing against it. Awmal sneered as the boys made their way toward the doorway.

"Let's put an end to this right now," said Hanniel. "Oops!" He swung

a sudden and swift arc with his sword in the direction of the armor just as

Danny slipped past it, and the whole thing crashed down with a loud CLANG.

Pieces fell off and bounced among the old stuff that was lying around. Then

from beyond the wall, they heard a loud shout:

"WHAT'S GOING ON IN THERE?"

Joey was the first to jump over the furniture and fly up the stairs,

dropping the flashlight as he ran with Danny close on his heels. But Mike

stopped, just for a moment. He turned and bent to pick up the flashlight,

squinting at the doorway. Did he see the dark outline of a figure ? He spun

around and ran out after the others.

Reverend David Palmer stepped out of the doorway into the room.

He sneezed from the dust and coughed before he could get any words out.

"Didn't I see you in church a couple of hours ago?" he sputtered,

but Mike had disappeared up the steps. The young pastor walked further

into the room and nearly tripped over a piece of armor. "No point in trying to

chase them," he said outloud after righting himself and wiping his nose with a

handkerchief. "They'll be out the back gate and down the street by now. I

definitely will have to replace that lock though." Pastor Palmer flipped on the

light, crossed the room, went up the stairs and pulled the doors closed. He

came back down and picked up the head piece of the old set of armor. "I

wonder if they'll be in church tomorrow. I'm sure I'll know them if I see

them again," he said smiling. "Especially the one in the choir with the bushy eyebrows."

"I certainly hope so," murmured Shamael in reply to the young pastor, who, of course, didn't hear him. He and Jediael looked over at Hanniel, who was still laughing at the comical way the boys flew up the stairs.

"I'll admit one thing," he said. "My Danny *was* wonderful. He was absolutely the best at getting out of here. And I hope that they didn't think a ghost knocked down that armor." The two other angels chuckled.

"Maybe they will, maybe they won't," said Shamael. "But I bet they won't be trespassing again anytime soon." Then Shamael quickly turned and pointed his sword straight at Awmal. He was still smiling, but his eyes became cold and hard.

"As for you - watch yourself!"

Awmal didn't answer but backed away still glowering. The three angels slipped through the wall leaving a pondering Pastor Dave standing in the middle of the room and an angry Awmal cowering in the corner.

* * * * * *

Meanwhile, Mike, Joey, and Danny were racing down the street out of the Palmer yard, across the lot, and between the houses. They were halfway up their block when they saw Rick Jeffries standing right in their way forcing them to slow down. They would have run around him had he not grabbed Mike and Joey by the sleeves.

"Where're you guys running from so fast - a bank robbery? Why don't you give me some of the money?"

"None of your business!" yelled Mike, as he and Joey shook themselves loose from his grip. "And we don't have any money!" Danny hung back a bit, and Joey stood glaring with his fists clenched. Mike stepped up between them and Rick. He would have been hard for one of them to tackle, but Mike knew he wouldn't try to fight all three of them at once.

"OK, OK, chill out," said Rick, as he looked over their heads at the path they just came from. "But what would your mommies say if they knew you were snooping around the Palmer place?" The three didn't answer him but took off running again, not stopping until they reached the Edward's home.

"Who was that?" asked Danny panting from the run.

"A jerk," replied Mike. "Forget him."

Chapter 3

Mike's Dilemma

The boys didn't have a chance to talk again until after dinner, and even then they couldn't say much with Teddy hanging around. Teddy looked like a smaller, chubbier version of Danny, but without the glasses. He was almost all of five years old and was always asking questions. Grownups called him 'precocious.' Joey called him "pest." Teddy could pluck anybody's last nerve, especially when he was minding everyone else's business.

"I know who won," said Teddy, loudly and right into Danny's ear.

"What?" said Danny with his face practically in the video game that Joey had finally let him play with.

"I *said* I know who won." Danny looked up.

"What are you talking about?"

Mike got a sinking feeling in his stomach, he could just imagine what was coming next. Teddy stood up straight and put his hands on his hips.

"You won. I saw you come in first when you guys were racing down the street."

Joey and Mike were sitting on the floor in front of the TV in Joey's room with their backs turned toward Danny and Teddy. Danny was sitting at a small table with the handheld game and Teddy had been peering over his shoulder.

"Where were you racing from?" asked Teddy.

"TEDDY!" said Danny now exasperated by both Teddy's nosiness and the game which he was losing. "For your information, we were NOT racing."

"Then why were you running?"

Joey looked at Mike and rolled his eyes toward the ceiling. Mike slapped his hand against his forehead. "Danny, you idiot," he wailed "Will you…"

"WHERE!!!" yelled Teddy, who now ran over and leaped onto Mike's back.

"I'll be back in a minute," said Joey, who got up and sprinted out of the room. Mike wrestled Teddy off his back and gave him a good tickling, hoping that it would take the little boy's mind off what he'd seen. Joey was back almost as soon as he was gone.

"Teddy," he said, "Dad wants you."

"Daddy called me?" said Teddy as he stood up, still panting.

"Yeah, hurry up," answered Joey.

"DADDY!" yelled Teddy, as he ran out of the room.

"Did Dad really call him?" asked Danny.

"I said he was trying to hog the Game Boy," said Joey with a shrug. Mike as always was amazed at how easily Joey could make up stuff like that and always in the nick of time, but he couldn't think about it for long. Now that Teddy was gone, the discussion turned to what had happened at the Palmer place.

"Do you think it really *was* a ghost?" asked Danny.

"I think it could be," answered Joey. "Mom said that when I was real little and we lived with my first dad, our next door neighbor was a lady who had lived around here for years." Joey lowered his voice for emphasis "She said that three people died in that house. One was an old woman who was sick, and then there was an old man."

"That was old man Palmer's father, right?" asked Mike.

"Yeah," said Joey. "And the last one…" he paused.

"What?" cried Danny "Tell me!"

"Was MURDERED!" said Joey, his eyes now wide as saucers.

"Wow!" said Danny, suddenly sitting bolt upright. "My grandma once said something about a man in that house, but she only shook her head about it and wouldn't say anything more."

"See?" said Joey, "Now I know something really did happen in there. And I bet it was his ghost that we heard in that basement."

"*And* who made the armor fall," added Danny.

"I don't know," said Mike. "It sounded to me like a real person who yelled out."

"But no one was there," insisted Danny. "They always go to visit their kids on the weekends and especially on holidays. My grandma said so."

"How do you know for sure?" answered Mike. "Couldn't it be that just this once somebody stayed home? And you know…wait a minute!" Mike slapped his forehead again. "When I was at choir rehearsal, some guy came in and talked to us. I think his name *was* something - or- other Palmer."

"I don't know," said Joey, leaning forward and rubbing his chin. "I still think it was a ghost, and I have a pretty good idea how we could find out for sure."

* * * * * *

Awmal smiled unseen from his perch on top of the chest of drawers. That was just what he wanted to hear, because he had a pretty good idea what Joey had in mind.

* * * * * *

Sunday morning found the boys with Joey's mom, Ms. Nina Edwards, at Community Fellowship Church. Mike sat on the end of the pew so he could go forward when it was time for the Youth Choir to go sit in the choir stand. Service hadn't started yet, but Teddy was already squirming and Joey was already bored.

"Mom," whined Joey. "Are we gonna have to sit through the whole thing? Can't we just leave after Mike and them sing?"

"Of course not, Joey," said Ms. Nina, pulling Teddy off the floor and back into his seat. "It's only polite to stay for the whole service. Besides, Danny and Teddy's mom asked that they go to church when they are visiting. Teddy, why can't you behave yourself like Danny?"

"Oh, he never sits still in church," said Danny, "even when we go with our grandma, and she takes us a lot."

"Yeah?" grumbled Joey. "I only have to come when you guys are here."

* * * * * *

"Really?" said Hanniel with half a smile at Jediael. "Not been to church for three weekends since Teddy and my Danny last visited? And just what have you been doing about this?" Shemael, Hanniel, Jediael and Teddy's angel Barrachel had taken their place with a host of others that stood guard unheard and unseen around the walls and above the pews. Many of them had young charges seated in the service below. The rest were there for the same reason as everyone else: to worship the Holy One. Jediael shrugged.

"I can only guard him; I can't make them bring him to church, unless you think I should borrow a thunderbolt from the Holy One and..."

"Shhh," said Shemael. "They're starting."

* * * * * *

The service started out the same as always. There was a long opening hymn, then a scripture reading, and then an even longer prayer. Then the choir sang. Joey was drawing pictures in his church bulletin, and by now, Teddy had dozed off. The offering plates had just been collected when Mike got the surprise of his life, as if Saturday's surprise had not been enough. The minister, Pastor Roberts, got up to give the announcements as usual, but then he said, "I'd like our friend, Pastor David Palmer to come up and say a few words of greeting. He and his wife will be in town for the next several months, and they will be helping us with our youth program."

A tall, youngish looking man with tanned skin, dark eyes, wavy hair and an engaging smile came to the podium and began to speak. Mike felt like his stomach suddenly leaped into his chest, and he sat straight up. Mike tried to catch Joey's eye, but he was still busy drawing and barely looked up. Of course both Joe and Danny were too far away to whisper to. Like any good speaker, Pastor Palmer scanned the audience as he spoke, but was there really a slight smile and a twinkle in his eye as he looked towards Mike? Mike scolded himself for being silly. "It's impossible," he said under his breath. "He couldn't have seen us. It was dark, and we weren't there that long, and he probably isn't even looking at me." Yet Mike couldn't shake the thought that the young minister did see and recognize him. Mike was staring at his shoes when Mrs. Roberts, who was sitting behind him, said, "What a lovely little speech." Mike, of course, didn't hear a word of it after he recognized the voice. Still he mustered up enough courage to sneak a glance as Pastor Palmer passed the choir to return to his seat. Mike's heart sank, the man definitely smiled at him.

After church nearly everyone stayed for awhile in the fellowship hall for cookies, punch, and conversation. The younger kids were running around, and Teddy was busy playing tag. Grownups stood around in groups of three or four, and Pastor and Mrs. Roberts were moving from group to group. Joey's mom and her friend Mrs. Perkins managed to corner Pastor and Mrs. Palmer and were soon huddled in conversation. Meanwhile, Joey stationed himself in a corner near a plate of cookies, but Mike edged towards Danny, who was standing nearby. Making sure he stayed out of Pastor Palmer's view, he caught Danny's eye and motioned for him to come over.

"You see that Palmer guy?" Mike asked.

"Yeah," replied Danny. "Joey's mom said he's old man Palmer's son.

"Does your grandma know him?"

"She knows old Mr. Palmer and even said she used to baby-sit for them, or something like that," Danny replied. He turned to walk towards the cookies, but Mike stopped him.

"Wait, remember when he was talking? Didn't he sound like the voice in the basement?"

Before Danny could say anything, Ms. Nina was calling them.

"Joey! Come here. Where's Danny and Teddy? You come too, Mike. Come and meet Reverend and Mrs. Palmer."

They all went over, but Mike hung back a bit. Pastor Palmer stuck out his hand.

"You guys can call me Pastor Dave." He shook hands with Joey, Teddy, and Danny in turn. Mike hesitated and stood to the side until they started to walk back towards Joey's mom. Pastor Dave then turned around to face Mike and took a step or two toward him while holding out his hand. Mike automatically raised his hand but then suddenly blurted out -

"Do you believe in ghosts?" Pastor Dave smiled as he shook Mike's hand.

"Was that what you were looking for?" he asked quietly. For a moment Mike wondered if anyone had ever really died of embarrassment.

In fact, if the floor could have opened up and swallowed him in an instant, it would have been OK. Since it didn't, he simply pulled his hand back without answering. Besides, no one else had even heard them because of what Joey's mom was saying to Mrs. April Palmer.

"My son Joey and his friend Mike attend church here all the time. Teddy and Danny will be visiting with us all summer. I'm sure that their mother will be happy to have them participate in your summer Vacation Bible School program."

"Mom, what are you doing this for?" Joey protested, when they were walking back to the minivan where Joey and Danny's dad was waiting to pick them up. "Why are you sentencing us to summer school at church?" He asked again after they were in the van, so his dad could hear.

"It's not summer school," Ms. Nina replied. "It's a two-week program. It will be good for you to go. Pastor Palmer will be in charge of it." She looked over at Mr. Edwards. He grumbled something but didn't really protest, and Joey sat back and scowled. The grownups continued their own conversation, so Mike leaned over to whisper to Joey.

"He saw us, you know."

"Who saw what?"

" It was Pastor Dave in the basement. He saw us when we ran out."

"How do you know?" whispered Joey, now surprised.

"He told me… sort of. Actually, he asked what we were looking for." (Mike left out the part when he asked Pastor Dave if he believed in ghosts).

"What did you say?"

"Well, nothing," admitted Mike.

"Then how do you really know if he saw anything? Did you at least ask if there was a ghost? Who would know more about a ghost in there than him? Except maybe Old Man Palmer."

"I wasn't gonna ask him all that," said Mike. "Besides, he looked at me like he already knew what we did."

"Remember, tomorrow we find out for sure," said Joey, as if he didn't even hear Mike's last comment.

"Find out what?"

"If there's really a ghost or not. And if that minister really saw us. "

"How?" asked Mike. But the mini van had just pulled up to his house.

"I'll tell you tomorrow," Joey replied, just before Mike shut the car door.

* * * * * *

Shamael looked over at Jediael, as the group floated silently above the minivan.

"What does Joey mean?" he asked.

"I'm not sure yet," replied Jediael, folding his arms. "I think I know though, and I don't like it."

Mike's Dilemma

Chapter 9

Mike's Dilemma

Memorial Day Monday started out sunny, but as the day moved into afternoon, clouds began to roll in. It didn't matter to Mike, Danny, and Joey, since they planned to be indoors anyway. The three were at Mike's house, seated around a table in the basement with most of the lights off. Only a grayish haze came in from the window above the table. Mike's dad, Mike Senior, had to work the holiday. Mr. Edwards took Joey's mom to the mall and then took Teddy to a kiddy movie. Mike's mom was using her day off to do some house cleaning. The boys were alone with only the distant sound of a vacuum cleaner whirring somewhere upstairs. Joey sat with a large brown paper bag on his lap.

"So, what's in the bag?" asked Danny. Without a word, Joey pulled out two objects. First, a folded board that had writing on it. It looked something like a table game with letters of the alphabet, numbers zero through nine, and the words yes and no as well as some other pictures. Then, he pulled out a plastic triangle with a hole in it and little legs that made it look like a miniature table.

"What it is?" asked Mike.

"It's a Ouija board" answered Joey.

"Where'd you get it?"

My mom's closet," said Joey. "Back when we were in the fourth grade, Dad and some of her friends gave her a birthday party, and somebody gave it to her as a gift. I sneaked out of my room and saw how they made it work."

"So, what are we supposed to do with it?" said Mike.

"Ask it questions," replied Joey. "Maybe it will tell us who the ghost in the basement is…I mean *was*."

"That wasn't a ghost," insisted Mike. "It was Pastor Dave. I remembered his voice in church, and he said he saw us."

"So, even if it was him, it still doesn't mean there isn't a ghost," said Joey. "You know all the stuff people say happened in there."

Mike didn't have an answer for that so Joey pressed further. "Did Pastor Dave say that there was no ghost in there?"

"No."

"Well, let's see if it'll tell us anything," said Joey, as he unfolded the board and put it in the center of the table and placed the triangle on top. He sat opposite Mike and put the fingertips of both hands on the triangle. "Ok, you put your hands on too - not hard, lightly."

"Then, do we ask it something?" Mike hesitated before he put his hands on the same as Joey.

"Yeah," said Joey. Danny bit his nails as he looked on.

"Guys, I think something is really wrong with this," he said finally.

"Yeah?" said Joey. "What?"

"I don't know."

"Are you being chicken again?" said Joey narrowing his eyes. "Cause if you are, you may as well just…"

"I AM NOT!" shouted Danny but then slapped the palm of his hand over his own mouth. All three boys froze for a moment. The vacuum was still whirring in the distance. Then the doorbell rang. Mike sighed.

"Just be quiet and watch, OK?" Danny nodded, but he still didn't look too certain.

"Ouija board, please tell us," said Joey slowly in a low voice. "Is there a ghost in the Palmer house?"

* * * * * *

Awmal sat (unseen as usual) underneath the table between the boy's knees. He hadn't seen the boy's angels, but he knew they had to be somewhere close by. No time to worry about that though. Nawgaf would stomp on him for sure if he didn't strike while he had the chance. He reached up through the table top and gave the triangle a slight push, which sent it sliding several inches across the board. All three boys jumped.

* * * * * *

"Did you move it?" asked Mike wide eyed.

"I didn't move it," said Joey. "I thought you moved it."

"But then who…" said Danny, but he was cut off mid-sentence by the sound of Mike's mom coming down the basement steps with Mrs. Ellen Edwards right behind her. She had gone by Joey's house to pick up Teddy and Danny. When no one was home, she crossed the street and rang the Bryant's bell. They were both in the room before anyone could move.

"What on earth! Mike, what are you boys doing down here in the dark?" said Mike's mom as she flipped on all the lights. "And where did you get this thing?" Mike pointed at Joey.

"It's my mom's," Joey said meekly. (Nobody ever dared cross Ms. Meg when she was angry).

"Does she know that you have it?" Meg demanded. Joey had to admit that she did not.

Then Mike's mom picked up the board and the plastic piece and looked over at Ms. Ellen.

"Let's all go upstairs," she said. The boys slowly climbed up behind the grownups, and Joey signaled his disappointment with a deep sigh. Danny looked relieved, but Mike wasn't sure just what to think. When they were all seated around the dining room table, the Ouija board closed on the table with the triangle piece on top, his mom started the lecture.

"Mike," she said, "you know that you have no business using anything like this - none of you should. And, Joey, you should know better than to take your mother's things without her knowing it."

"But, Mom," said Mike, "we were just playing with it, like a game."

"Yeah, Mrs. Bryant," added Joey, "it wasn't anything serious."
The phone rang. Ms. Meg excused herself and went to answer it.

"But, Joey," continued Mrs. Ellen Edwards, "that just isn't true. What you boys were doing could be very dangerous. Why would you even want to play with something like this?"

"We wanted to know if there was a ghost at the Old Palmer house," said Danny. Mike and Joey exchanged glances. Would Danny spill the beans?

"Danny," his mom answered, "The Bible says 'absent from the body, present with the Lord.' Now old Mr. David Palmer who died in that house, I know he was a true Christian man. That means his spirit went straight to God when he died and would certainly not be waiting around for you boys to come visit. As for people who don't know God, well, some folks say that if someone dies a bad death, their ghost may remain around the place where they died. But the Bible doesn't say anything like that. It does say in the Gospel of Luke, where Jesus told the parable about the rich man and Lazarus, that the rich man died and went to Hades. He couldn't even speak to his brothers who were still alive, so no ghost is going to talk through a Ouija board. But, most importantly, in the Bible God tells us that we should never, ever try to do things like talk to ghosts - not even for fun."

"But then why did the triangle thing move?" asked Joey.

"Yeah, Mom," said Danny "It did move - honest!" Mike sat up in his chair. He wanted to hear her answer to this.

"That triangle is called a planchette, and yes, I do believe you," Ms. Ellen replied. "You see, the Bible also says that a long, long time ago there was a very important angel, who was named Lucifer. But he got proud, so proud that he thought he was good enough to take God's place. God put him out of heaven for that, and from then on he was called Satan or the Devil. But when he left, he took a third of all the angels with him. They all turned bad, and now we call them evil spirits, or demons. These evil spirits know how much God loves us, so they try do things to pull us away from Him and keep us from doing what God wants us to do. They may even try to trick us into believing things that aren't true."

"So a demon might make a Ouija board work?" asked Danny. Ellen nodded.

Mike was just opening his mouth to say something when suddenly his mom returned to the room with a grim look on her face.

"That was Pastor Roberts," she said, looking straight at Mike. He said that the visiting minister saw you and two other boys in his basement on Saturday. Is that true?"

Mike's mouth was still open, but nothing came out. Joey looked at the floor. Danny looked like he was about to cry.

"Danny," said Ms. Ellen gently, "do you have something you need to say? Is this true?"

Danny nodded, and a big tear started to roll down his cheek. Suddenly, the doorbell rang again. When Meg opened the door, Teddy came bounding in with Ms. Nina close behind.

"I'm back from the mall," she said cheerily, "and Teddy's been telling me all about the movie... hey why's everybody so glum. Did I miss a funeral or something?"

Meg went to the dining room table, picked up the Ouija board and planchette, and then brought them back to where Nina was standing.

"Joey admits that he took these out of your room." she said.

"And," added Ms. Ellen, who was still seated at the table with the boys, "the pastor just called to say that they were playing inside the Palmer house without permission."

"Oh... well, was he really mad or something?" said Ms. Nina.

"Who? Pastor Roberts?" asked Meg.

"Well, him too, but I mean, Dave Palmer?"

"No, the Pastor didn't say that," said Ms. Meg, "but he did want us to know."

"Oh, well," said Ms. Nina with a little laugh, taking the Ouija board and tucking it under her arm. "I guess boys will be boys. Teddy and Danny's duffel bag is all packed," she added to Ms. Ellen. "I'll bring it out to you." Joey jumped up and followed his mom as she turned to go. Ms. Meg and Ms. Ellen looked at each other and then back at Ms Nina.

"Oh, hey,'" said Nina over her shoulder. "I'm really sorry about all this. I'm sure it won't happen again. Come on you," she said to Joey scolding him as they walked out the door. "Didn't I tell you about bothering my things?"

When she was gone, Ellen rose and took both Danny and Teddy by the hand.

"You and I are gonna have a long talk with the Lord this evening," she said to Danny who was looking at his shoes. "Then we'll talk about how to discipline you for this.

Take care, Meg," she called back as they walked towards the car.

"I'm sure Nina will mention all this to Greg."

Meg slowly closed the door and turned back to Mike.

"I believe you have a lot to think about," she said. "I'm not saying anything more until I talk to your father." Then without another word, she picked up the vacuum hose, turned on the machine and went back to her cleaning. Mike wandered back downstairs and sat down at the table, where he was sitting when they got caught. His mom usually yelled at him when she was mad, but her silent treatment was even worse.

"Dad will kill me for sure," he muttered out loud. "Some holiday." He sat mulling things over for a few more minutes, until he heard his mom dragging the vacuum down the stairs. Suddenly, he noticed something white on the floor near the table and picked it up. It was the instruction sheet to the Ouija board that had fallen unnoticed out of Joey's bag, which was still by the side of the chair. By now, his mom was down the steps, and was about to plug in the vacuum.

"Don't you think that your room is the best place for you right now?" she said, without looking up.

"Sure, Mom," he answered. Mike quickly stuffed the paper into his pocket and ran up the stairs.

* * * * * *

Shamael watched the whole scene from the far corner of the dining room.

"Do you think that will be the end of it?" asked Jediael from his post across the street.

"Of the Ouija board?" replied Shamael. "Maybe. Unfortunately, temptation is always around." He then pointed his sword towards Awmal who was still under the basement table. "Out!"

Awmal didn't have to be told twice.

Mike's Dilemma

Chapter 5

Mike's Dilemma

"Wow," said Danny thoughtfully. "So we shouldn't play with that Ouija board ever again."

"Never," said Pastor Dave. It was Sunday after church two weeks later. Mike, Joey, and Danny were in the church study listening to Pastor Dave expound on Ouija boards and the like across the huge expanse of Pastor Robert's desk. He not only reiterated everything Danny's mom told them, but he added more stuff of his own. Joey stifled a yawn, but Mike shifted uncomfortably in his seat. Not a day went by in the past two weeks that he didn't hear something about the basement incident or the Ouija board incident. His dad, Mike Sr., was less upset about the Ouija board and more concerned with their going into the Palmer house. "A body could get shot for trespassing!" he yelled. "Do you think I work this hard for you to amount to nothing, boy?" And on and on it went. His mom didn't shout as much, but she started saying things about Mike "spending more time in church."

At his dad's suggestion, she called the Palmer house to apologize for Mike's part in the whole affair and to make amends. To Meg's surprise, Pastor Palmer was not only glad to hear from her but invited the three boys to the church to meet with him and talk about it as soon as Danny could visit again. So after two weeks of torture (Both Mike and Danny were sentenced to two weeks of no TV and even Joey had to give up his beloved video games for a whole weekend), the boys and their dads were ushered into the

Pastor's study. Mr. Edwards and Mike Bryant, Sr. said that the boys wanted to apologize and make things right. Both ministers listened, and then Pastor Roberts asked them if they would step outside with him for a bit. When they were gone, Pastor Dave slid into the big chair behind the desk, rested his chin in his hand, leaned forward and gazed at each of them.

"What do you have to say for yourselves?" Mike sighed with the biggest sigh of his life and told the whole story, starting with their decision to look for the ghost. He ended with the Ouija board and what Danny's mom had to say about it.

"We're sorry," Mike said as he finished. "It was dumb and we shouldn't have done it." That's what launched Pastor Dave into his lecture. Unlike Mike Sr., the young pastor seemed more concerned with the Ouija board than even their being in his basement without permission. He ended his talk in a very serious tone, "Guys, you've done something very dangerous. There is a reason why that Ouija board seemed to work, and, Danny, your mom may be right: it's very possible that an evil spirit was responsible. It's their job to do everything that they can do to keep people from coming to Jesus Christ or to keep them from being all the best that God wants them to be."

Mike made a face.

"That's even creepier than ghosts!" Pastor Dave smiled, but then he became serious again.

"Playing with that stuff or doing anything that has to do with the

Occult can practically invite demon powers right into your life. He waited a moment for that thought to sink in and then turned to Joey. "I've heard what Mike and Danny had to say. What about you?" Joey shrugged.

"My mom says a Ouija board is only a game and what's the big deal about it." (Mike could have sworn that Joey almost smiled as he spoke.) But then he looked at the floor. "But my dad's really mad about us going into your basement. Sorry." Pastor Dave rested his chin in his hand again and looked at Joey for long time. Then his face brightened.

"We'll have more time later to talk about this, but listen. My mom and dad, my sister, and my wife April and I will be in that house all summer. We have big plans for the old place that we think will help this whole community. In addition to all the repairs that are going on, we'll need to spend lots of time cleaning it out, especially that junk in the basement. With your parents permission, I'd like you boys to come Saturdays after school's out to help with the clean-up, and, Mike, I'd like you to be in charge of the three of you. I also expect your full participation and model behavior when the summer Youth Program starts in a couple of weeks. Do this, and I'll consider us square with what happened on that Saturday before Memorial Day. Is it a deal?" All three of them chimed in "Deal". Pastor Dave shook hands all round and walked over to open the door. Mike Sr. and Mr. Greg both stepped back in with Pastor Roberts close behind. Pastor Dave shook hands with their dads.

"I think things will work out just fine. And, Mr. Bryant, thanks for your idea about having the boys help us clean up the mansion. If you folks agree, I'd like the boys to start the first Saturday after school's out." Both men nodded and Pastor Dave added, "And we hope to see you both in church with the boys this Sunday?" Mike Sr. smiled but shook his head.

"Well, I'd like to but it's awful hard with working two jobs and all. But I think this youth program and the Saturday thing will be just what we need to keep these boys busy. Don't you think so, Greg?"

"Sure thing," said Mr. Edwards, as he put his hand on Joey's and Danny's shoulders, and they all turned to go. For some reason though, Mike had a strange urge, and just before he went out the door, he turned and put out his hand again to Pastor Dave. He took it, but this time he held it for a few moments, looking Mike straight in the eye. They smiled at each other, and Mike ran out to catch up with the others.

* * * * * *

Awmal however was far from pleased. He and Nawgaf also been watching the whole thing but from some distance away. Awmal was worried that Nawgaf might think he struck out a third time. After all, he didn't make much progress in either the Palmer house or the Bryant house, and now Mike and his friends would be spending more time with the young minister than ever.

"All is not lost," said Nawgaf, answering his unspoken thought.

"What?"

"You heard me. Despite your incompetence there is still a chance if your efforts are better placed. For example, you won't get too far with the one called Danny."

"You don't think so?" answered Awmal.

"He prays, his mother prays, not to mention those grandparents of his. They never stop." Nawgaf folded his arms and shook his head. "No, leave others to trouble him. You concentrate on the one called Mike. I believe that he can yet be turned from that other cause."

"What about the one called Joey?" asked Awmal.

"Him?" said Nawgaf with a snort. "Don't waste your time. At the rate he's going, he won't need our help."

Mike's Dilemma

Jannette Morrow

Chapter 6

Mike's Dilemma

Finally, school year was over, and graduation went off without a hitch. Mike managed to walk across the stage and collect his commendations (one for attendance, one for good citizenship and one for math) without tripping or otherwise making an idiot out of himself. Joey, of course, managed to almost trip the person next to him, but that was on purpose and strictly for laughs. There was even a small get together in the Bryant's backyard for ice cream and cake after the ceremony for Mike, Joey, and a couple of other kids in the class despite the basement incident. Corrie Thompson came with her cousin Kate and Sunnie Powers was there too. Of course, Pastor and Mrs. Roberts, and Pastor and Mrs. Palmer were invited, and to Mike and Joey's surprise, they actually came. But like all good things, the day ended and as promised, that first Saturday after school was out, the three boys were sweeping up dust and mopping floors in the back rooms of the Palmer mansion. Mike complained to his dad. "It's musty and dusty, and we had to work for three hours straight!"

"Good for you," replied Mike Sr. without looking up from his newspaper. Shamael silently agreed.

Fourth of July came and went, and that following Monday, the kids of Community Fellowship Church began the two week summer Vacation Bible School program. Devotion and Bible study were in the morning, but after lunch Pastor Dave called the whole group into the fellowship hall.

"OK, guys, listen up," he said. "One of our goals for the youth at Community Fellowship will be raising money for missionary work. Anyone have any good ideas?" Joey jabbed Mike with his elbow.

"I dare you to raise your hand," he whispered through a guffaw. Kate Thompson raised hers.

"Aren't we supposed to be doing arts and crafts in the afternoons? Why don't we just like make stuff that we can sell?"

"Wonderful!" said Pastor Dave, "and for such a great idea, Kate, you can have the honor of being in charge of selling. Any other ideas?" Pastor Dave looked around the room. Joey grabbed Mike's hand and thrust it in the air.

"Hey, Mike, I was hoping you would volunteer. What's your idea?" Mike's cheeks burned while Joey fell over laughing and several other kids laughed too. Mike shoved Joey and rolled his eyes. He was just about to protest, but he caught sight of a Flannel graph in the corner where the nursery class had Sunday school the day before. An old sock puppet still lay in the corner on the floor.

"I dunno. Maybe we could do a puppet show." Mike looked again at the flannel graph. Fabric sheep and people were still stuck on the light blue felt background. "Maybe we could like, do a Bible story. We could make the stuff for it in arts and crafts, like the stuff for sale." Mike snickered at his own idea. It was so corny that he wasn't even mad when mostly everyone giggled. Pastor Dave had a huge grin on too.

"Excellent," he said, pulling Mike up to his feet, and putting his arm around his shoulder. "OK, everybody here knows Mike. He will be in charge of the puppet show." Pastor Dave then beckoned Kate to stand up too. "Now, first, I want everybody to give it up for Mike and Kate for volunteering their time and talent." Pastor Dave paused while all the kids clapped and hooted. "Next, everyone who wants to sell go over and sit with Kate, and everyone who wants to work on the show, come over and stand here with Mike. All of our youth workers will be available to help you guys get organized. Let's get to work." Mike was still embarrassed, but in a funny way, this was even better than being elected class vice-president.

Every afternoon for two weeks was spent making puppets, writing a script, making and collecting stuff to sell, and deciding who would do what. They even built a puppet stage from cardboard boxes and a few pieces of wood. Everything was ready by Friday afternoon. About half of the kids, including Mike, Danny, and Joey, set up for the Bible story puppet show. The rest arranged the arts and crafts, the donations from parents, and the cookies and lemonade that would be for sale. The Youth Program /Vacation Bible School Fair in the church backyard was about ready to begin.

"Joey, will you stop clowning around!" shouted Mike. He and Danny had just set up the cardboard puppet stage when Joey who was spinning like a top nearly knocked it down.

* * * * * *

"I suppose being in charge is a lot harder than he thought it would be," murmured Jediael to Shamael.

"Isn't it always?" Shamael replied. The angels watched as Pastor Roberts came and stood near Pastor Dave.

"So, how's it going?"

"OK, so far," replied Pastor Dave. "Everybody has worked really hard for the fair. The older kids have been great in taking the lead. Especially Mike."

"Yes," answered Pastor Roberts. "That kid's got a lot of potential. There's a great future for him, if he stays on track."

Shamael looked around and smiled an invisible smile. Every kid in the church lot was at work, and everyone had an angel that was looking out for him or her. All of it was in honor of the Holy One, and it would please Him if the fair were successful. At the same time however, Awmal, Nawgaf, and every other evil spirit that was crawling around knew the same thing. Shamael knew for a fact that they were out to mess things up the best they could. He silently unsheathed his sword and watched Awmal inch closer to Nawgaf, who stood in a corner of the yard observing dozens of demons scurrying back and forth.

"Have you been following my instructions?" asked Nawgaf without looking away from the scene in front of him.

"I've been trying to," Awmal whined "but it seems he's been spending time with that new - that new…"

"That pastor?"

"Yes," replied Awmal. He's been sending up prayers for the boy - makes it harder to get at him."

"You heard my orders. Don't try; do it! We can't afford to let this one get away. Besides, you know my plan." Nawgaf shifted his gaze to another corner of the yard where a solitary figure of a teenage girl was standing just outside the fence. He stared back at Awmal. "Don't ruin it," he said before slithering away towards the other demons.

* * * * * *

The children really transformed the yard into something that resembled a fair. Everyone who was at church that day came out to see, even the church secretary and the Helping Hands club that met at the church most Friday afternoons. Several people from the neighborhood wandered in, as well as the parents who didn't have to work that day. Danny, Kate, Corrie, and several other kids with puppets on both hands were kneeling or crouched behind the small stage. The kids from the pre K and kindergarten classes were just sitting down on the grass in front and a number of visitors, who had all paid a quarter for the privilege, were waiting for them to start. Mike was also in the back, bent down low so as not to be seen out front, his nose in the narration sheet which he was getting ready to read. Joey was crouched in front of him with his hand on the string to open the curtain. Everyone was concentrating so hard on his or her puppet that they barely noticed how close together they were.

"The puppet show that we will be performing today is titled 'Jesus and Lazarus'," began Mike while Joey slowly opened the curtain. "This story is found in the Gospel of John, the eleventh chapter…" Things went smoothly enough until the part where Jesus returned from staying away two extra days.

"Jesus," Kate made her puppet Mary say, "if you had been here, my brother would not have died." Reggie Matthews with his bandaged-wrapped Lazarus Inside the Tomb crouched down, ready to move his puppet forward at the right time. Mike was leaning right over Joey, who was right behind Reggie.

"Lazarus!" Danny made his puppet Jesus say, "Come …" Mike never knew how he fell over onto Joey causing him to bump into Reggie right at that precise moment. Lazarus came forth in a hurry, along with Reggie's entire arm to the delight of the four and five- year-olds who were watching. Everyone jumped, and in an instant the whole thing toppled into the audience with six kids on top.

"WHAT THE HECK ARE YOU DOING?" Joey yelled as they fell.

"It was an accident!" Mike shouted back . "I didn't mean to fall in!" Kids ran in every direction, and nobody understood what Reggie was saying, since his mouth was full of cardboard. Pastor Dave and Mrs. Roberts ran in to help everyone up, and fortunately no one was really hurt. Mike's first thought was to run someplace and hide, and he almost did. But then he thought of what his dad and Pastor Dave too would think of him if he ran away. So he stood up, took a deep breath, stepped over Joey, who was by now doubled up on the ground laughing, and started to pick up the now smashed cardboard stage. The four and five-year-olds (who, miraculously, got away) were also laughing, along with all the puppeteers who had fled the scene. All except for Reggie, who was currently being escorted inside by Mrs. Roberts to get a band-aid for his elbow. As he lugged the stage towards the end of the yard, Mike could have sworn that even every grown-up he passed was suppressing a smile. He was too embarrassed to even look at Pastor Dave, who was still calming everyone down and making sure all the other kids were all right.

Mike walked to the storage shed near the fence where the re-cycle trash and garbage cans were kept, but he didn't notice the girl who was still standing there, until she spoke.

"Hi, Mike," she said in a sweet singsong sort of voice. Mike looked up startled.

"Who're you?" The girl giggled, and her smile seemed to light up her pretty coffee with extra cream colored face. She had long straight black hair with a bit of curl at the ends, and her eyes were grayish green.

"Don't you remember me? I'm Venetia Powers; my sister was in your class. I was in the car when we came by your house after the elementary school graduation." Mike didn't remember seeing Venetia at the party, but it was easy to see her resemblance to Sunnie. Yet she was older, taller, and somehow more glamorous. He was surprised and even a bit flattered.

"How come you remember me?"

"Cause you're cute," she replied, flashing him a smile. "Besides, Sunnie said you were class vice president. It was really brave of you to stay and pick up your puppet stage like that."

Mike started to feel his cheeks burning. Just then Joey sidled up next to him.

"Hey, Venetia," he said brightly, "What's up? Where's Sunnie?"

"Hey, Joey," she returned. "Sunnie's at my mom's apartment downtown. Now that school's out, it's my turn to stay out here with our grandmother, at least for the next few weeks. "So," she added, "is this where you guys go to church?"

"Yeah," returned Joey. How'd you know?"

"Me and my mom saw Danny's mom at the supermarket," Venetia replied. She turned briefly to Mike adding, "We live on the other side of Chesterton in the Dawson Garden Apartments. My mom's place is in the same circle as Danny, Teddy and their mom." Turning back to Joey, she went on. "Anyway, they were talking, and Mrs. Edwards said that Danny and Teddy went to a church with you guys called Community Fellowship when they come to visit their dad out here." Venetia giggled again. "She said that I should check it out if I was going to be here for the summer, and come to find out, my grandmother comes here too. Is Danny around?"

"He's here," Joey replied, pointing backwards with his thumb over his shoulder. Mike watched the conversation is silence, looking from Joey to

Venetia in turn. Suddenly she smiled at him again.

"Well, I gotta go, grandma's waiting. I guess you guys will be with Sunnie at Central Junior High in September?"

"Yup!" answered Joey. Mike could only nod.

"Ok, then," she said. "See you around" Venetia flipped her hair over her shoulder, and with a little wave at them, she started down the street.

"Y-you know her?" asked Mike, still stunned that anyone that looked anything like Venetia Powers would think he was brave - and cute!

"Like she said," replied Joey with a shrug. "Danny lives in her circle. We see her and her mom all the time when we take Danny and Teddy back home on Sunday nights. She's super popular. Her boyfriend is Cal McKay, and they hang around with all the cool kids in high school."

"McKay?" said Mike. "I've heard that name before."

"Everybody around here has heard it," returned Joey. "His dad's one of the richest guys in town. I know 'cause my dad works for Cal's dad at McKay Industries."

"I've seen Sunnie at church sometimes, but never Venetia." said Mike.

"That's because Sunnie mostly lives with their grandmother. But, you know, Danny's mom is always trying to talk to Sunnie and Venetia's mom about church and God and stuff. My dad says he doesn't even know why she tries, since they're a totally different religion. C'mon. Let's go back in and see if there's any cake left." Mike slowly followed Joey back to the others. What on earth could Joey mean by "a totally different religion"?

* * * * * *

Awmal watched the whole thing and saw Joey when he started to stroll towards Mike and Venetia at the fence. He began to move in that direction but was suddenly stopped by an exceptionally hard blow to the side of his green head. Awmal looked up only to see Jediael with a sword in his hand and a cool smile on his face. "Somebody just prayed for them," the angel said in an icy tone. And at that moment, all of the spirit beings could hear someone say "...in the name of Jesus amen." The very mention of the name of Jesus struck Awmal like a bat hitting a fly ball. Obviously, there would be no success - at least not right then. "Sooner or later," he hissed over his shoulder as he slunk away "someone will leave an opening, and I'll be ready."

"So will we," shot back Shamael from his position just behind Jediael. Awmal gave the angels a parting glare and turned to go, but not before glancing over again at Mike and Joey talking to the pretty girl over the fence. "I know Nawgaf said not to waste time on Joey" he muttered half to himself and half to the watching angels "but I bet he'll be just the one that I can use to get to the others. Especially that Mike."

Chapter 7

Mike's Dilemma

Shamael heard Pastor Dave say that particular prayer. And the next day, heard him tell his wife April that as much as he liked those other two he was glad for a chance to talk to Mike by himself, since Joey and Danny would be out with their dad that particular Saturday. A few minutes later, Mike and Pastor Dave were working in the dim light of a few old lamps in the basement. They were sorting through all sorts of cool stuff - baseballs with signatures on them, bats, and stacks of old baseball cards. There were several dusty chairs and sofas, boxes full of old clocks, cameras, books, and china. There was even a stack of old comic books. But despite all the interesting things there, Mike seemed preoccupied with his own thoughts. Finally, Pastor Dave sat down on one of the old sofas and patted the seat next to him for Mike to sit down.

* * * * * *

"Mike, for weeks you've been bugging me about this stuff down here, but now that you have a better chance to see it, you don't seem interested at all. You want to tell me what's on your mind?"

"I dunno," said Mike, looking down with a slight shrug. "Yesterday, I guess."

"Ah," said Pastor Dave. "The rise and fall of Lazarus the puppet." Mike smiled a little at the pun in spite of himself. "Don't feel bad," Pastor Dave continued. "You still did a great job, and you're a good leader too.

You came up with a good idea and carried it through. And you didn't run away when things went badly. That was brave."

Mike looked up.

"That's what Venetia said."

"Venetia? That's the Powers girl, isn't she? Pastor Roberts introduced me to her grandmother Mrs. Powers. Said she had two granddaughters and the oldest was sixteen. I saw you and Joey talking to her yesterday."

"Joey talked mostly," Mike admitted. "Her sister Sunnie was in me and Joey's class, and their mom lives near Danny. Joey says they're some other religion."

"Is that so? Well..." Pastor Dave's voice trailed off for a second, and he started sorting through another box.

"Tell me about Joey. You've been friends long?"

"Yeah," said Mike. "First, I met him when our moms went to nursing school together. But we started being best friends in the third grade." Pastor Dave rested his chin in his hand.

"What is it with Joey?" he asked with a hint of a smile. "He's a bit of a trouble maker, isn't he?"

"Yeah. But everybody likes him. He's always making people laugh by telling jokes and doing stuff, and everybody always looks to see what he's going to do next."

"Do people ever notice you like that?" asked Pastor Dave, still smiling.

"No, I'm just regular, I guess," replied Mike, looking back down at his shoes, too embarrassed to mention that Venetia seemed to notice him. "Nobody but Rick, and he's always trying to push us around. My mom and dad say ignore him but it's hard when he's always calling us mean names and trying to take our money." Pastor Dave leaned back and crossed his arms over his chest.

"You know," he said, "when God made us, he gave each person his or her own special personality, and he made everybody good at something. He seems to have given Joey a talent for getting people's attention. Now, that can be a good thing if you're showing them something good. But it can go all wrong if getting attention becomes more important than doing what is right. Do you understand?"

"I think so," said Mike. Pastor Dave went on.

"As for Rick, well, I haven't met him yet, so I can't be sure what his talent is. I'm sure he has one; he just has to learn to use it, and then he wouldn't need to be a bully. You may not seem to get a lot of attention now, but I think that God has some very special things in store for you. If you give Him your whole life, not only will He bring out the best of your natural talents, but He will give you His Holy Spirit to help you and give you special talents called gifts."

Mike began to shift uneasily and picked at an imaginary piece of lint on his jeans. This was starting to sound like the invitation at church. He changed the subject back to Venetia and Sunnie.

"If Sunnie's mom and Venetia are not our religion, then what are they?"

"Well," said Pastor Dave "first of all, Christianity is more than just religion; it's about having a real relationship with Jesus Christ. That's why He died on the cross.

It started when Adam and Eve disobeyed God in the Garden of Eden. Ever since then, every person born would be born a sinner, would eventually disobey God, and eventually would have to die because of it, since God is absolutely perfect, holy, and just. He can never accept us in our sin, but he still loves us immensely, nevertheless. When Jesus, who is God's son and the only perfectly sinless human being, willingly died on the cross for our sins, God accepted his death in place of ours. And because Jesus rose from the dead and lives forever, we can too. If we ask God to forgive us and accept Jesus Christ into our hearts, we can have the relationship with God that He always wanted to have with us. And that's not just while we're alive on earth, but afterwards in Heaven too. I don't know what religion Venetia and her mom are, but if it is not a true relationship with Jesus, they can never even hope to get to Heaven." Mike was silent for a moment while he considered that somber thought.

"You mean that everybody that doesn't accept Jesus is gonna go ..." Mike pointed downward with his thumb "down there?"

"That's what the Bible says," said Pastor Dave quietly. "Mike," he continued "what about you? Have you ever really asked God to forgive your sins and asked Jesus into your heart?"

Mike jumped up like a kernel of popcorn that had just popped.

"Can I ask my mom first? Besides, it's kind of musty down here - I think I need some air."

"OK," said Pastor Dave still seated. "It's about time for you to go anyway. But promise me that you'll keep thinking about it. And remember, when Vacation Bible School is over, the Summer Youth program will still meet every Wednesday afternoon and Friday night until the end of August. I'm hoping to see you guys there, and maybe you should invite Venetia and her sister too. And try being nice to Rick - maybe he's just a friend you haven't made yet."

"Sure," said Mike. He was glad for an excuse to talk to Venetia again even if he wasn't so sure about being nice to Rick. Pastor Dave got up and the two mounted the stairs and walked to the side door. Mike went out and started down the steps but then suddenly turned around.

"Do you really think I'm a good leader?" he asked.

"You bet," said Pastor Dave. "And so does the Lord." Mike walked down a step or two before he turned and started to ask Pastor Dave how he knew what God was thinking. But by then, the door had already closed.

* * * * * *

Shamael, on the other hand, had no doubts as to how the young pastor could know. He did wonder though if Pastor Dave had any inkling of the fight that had just gone on in the spirit world. Awmal alone was no match for him, but Awmal and Nawgaf together? Now that was a different story.

Mike's Dilemma

Shamael had fought those two for the whole time that Mike was at the Palmer home. Mike still hadn't made up his mind, but there were no disruptions by the demons thanks to Shamael's presence and his swift sword. Now at least Mike would have a chance to think long and hard about the things that Pastor Dave had told him. It was a tough fight though, tough enough that Shamael almost needed help. It was obvious that the two demons had specifically targeted Mike, and Shamael agreed with Pastor Dave's hunch that it was all about Mike's future and what God would do with it.

Jannette Morrow

Chapter 8

Mike's Dilemma

Vacation Bible School part of the Youth Program was now ended, but Mike couldn't get Venetia off his mind, or Pastor Dave either, for that matter. In fact, after that conversation on Saturday, Mike started taking more notice of the young minister. Mike watched the careful way he led the scripture reading that Sunday and noticed that Pastor Dave paid close attention when Pastor Roberts was preaching. On Wednesday after the youth program was over, Mike even spied Pastor Dave and Pastor Roberts in a corner of the church with their arms around each others' shoulders, heads bowed. For his part, Mike only prayed "Now I lay me down to sleep" when he went to bed. He wondered why anyone would pray in the middle of the day when there wasn't even a church service going on. Even so, Pastor Dave really did seem to have something special about him, and he in turn thought Mike was special too.

"Pastor Dave is nowhere as old as Pastor Roberts, but he is always praying," Mike mentioned to his parents one night during supper. "He can be lots of fun, but he gets real serious when he is talking about God. He told me that I should give my life to Jesus because God has something for me to do."

"He's a praying man, who has the hand of God on him" said Mike's dad. "I may not be much of a church-goer, but I always respect an honest preacher." Mike's mom, who seemed to be taking more interest in church since the Ouija board incident, was more thoughtful.

"Maybe the Lord really does have something special for you to do with your life, and he wants Pastor Dave to help guide you," she said.

Mike still had his talk with Pastor Dave on his mind when he, Danny, and Joey were in the basement that next Saturday bagging the trash that Pastor Dave and his wife had separated from the "good stuff" that they planned to keep. In the trash, they noticed some small, yellowed, and water-damaged leaflets that had the title "The Way to Salvation." Danny picked up one and started to read. Mike looked at it over Danny's shoulder and then looked over at Joey.

"When I was here last week, I told Pastor Dave what you said about Sunnie, Venetia, and their mom being another religion. He said everyone should accept Jesus into their heart or else they won't go to Heaven."

"Did you?" asked Danny, looking up at Mike.

"Did I what?"

"Ask Jesus to come into your heart." Mike shrugged.

"I dunno - kinda, I guess. You?"

"Oh, I prayed and asked Him to come into my heart when I was five years old. My grandma showed me how," replied Danny.

"Teddy, too?"

"Yep," said Danny. "And he was only four when he did." Mike wondered if that was why Danny was such a "goody good."

"Do you ever do anything really bad?" he asked.

"Well, first time we came here was bad, and so was playing with the Ouija board. But then me and my mom prayed and I asked Jesus to forgive me. And on the last day of school, I ate almost a whole jar of cookies and gave some to Teddy so he wouldn't tell." Danny smiled and looked down. "That night we both had to pray it."

"What about you, Joey?" asked Mike. Joey straightened up from tying closed one of the trash bags. He sucked his teeth and rolled his eyes.

"I dunno. Every time we go to church they talk about that stuff, and still half the time, nobody goes up. My dad says that even when people do go up to join church, they still do the same stuff everybody else does."

"But," protested Danny, "my grandma says that it's about more than just joining church. A person really has to ask Jesus to come into their heart. Then Jesus will change them, and then they really can be different."

"Well, maybe," replied Joey, "but my mom says that God loves everybody, and He mostly just wants us to live a good life. She says how can God send millions of people to Hell just because they don't believe in Jesus? What if they never heard of him?"

"But that's why my grandma became a missionary so she could help tell everybody."

"But, Danny," said Joey, who now seemed more interested in the topic, "remember that time last spring vacation when we brought you and Teddy home, and your mom was talking to Venetia, Sunnie, and their mom? Remember how Ms. Powers said that there are lots of different religions in the world and all of them help people to find God?"

"Yeah," said Danny, looking down again at the old tract. "But my mom still said that only Jesus can save us from our sins."

Joey only shrugged at this, but now Mike was more curious than ever. He wondered if there really was something to this whole church and salvation business. It seemed to work for Pastor Dave, Pastor Roberts and for Danny and Teddy too. But what about those 'other religions' that Joey kept referring to? And, more importantly, what did Venetia know about them? Mike wondered that if he asked her about it, maybe he could get her to notice him again. And what would happen to him if he did accept Jesus into his heart like Pastor Dave said? Could there really be something he was supposed to do for God? Mike's thoughts, as well as their conversation, were cut short when Mrs. April Palmer came downstairs to tell them that work time was over, and that ice cream and cookies were waiting for them upstairs.

"You'd better hurry, Mike," she added after they were seated, "because choir practice starts in an hour. I'll be helping Mrs. Roberts today, so we can walk over together. Joey, you and Danny can come too if you like."

An hour or so later, the sixteen choir members who were not away for the summer sat in the choir stand at church giggling and whispering to each other. Joey and Danny who did decide to tag along sat in the rear of the church along with various parents and siblings who were waiting for choir members. Mrs. Roberts began to pound away on the piano while Mrs. Palmer worked to keep order and to get the choir to sound right. Rather, she worked to get the boys to sound right. The girls pretty much had the right idea.

"OK," Mrs. Palmer said finally. "It looks like each of you guys will have to come up to the piano individually. It's the only way you'll get the part." So, one by one, each boy had to stand next to the piano and sing while Mrs. Roberts played until he got the tune. Naturally, it was all a hoot to everyone except the grownups. And, of course, Joey had to get into the act from the back of the church, making faces at the choir, pretending to sing, and sticking his fingers in his ears when someone was particularly off key. The kids laughed so loud that Pastor Roberts stuck his head out of his office to see what was going on. A few stern words from him calmed everybody down, and then it was Mike's turn. He nervously shuffled over to the piano, determined to get it over with. Mike was so nervous that he practically sang under his breath prompting a "Can you sing a little louder please?" from Mrs. Palmer. Suddenly, a wicked thought crossed Mike's mind. Pastor Roberts had already gone back into his office so why should Joey get all the laughs? So Mike took a deep breath and for the first time in his life sang at the top of his lungs. But instead of laughing, everybody just stared at him, Mrs. Palmer, Mrs. Roberts, all the kids, even Pastor Roberts, who actually came back into the room. Danny had a big grin, and Joey's mouth was wide open. Suddenly, somebody began to clap, and then everybody applauded. Once again, Mike felt his cheeks burning.

"Michael," said Mrs. Roberts (She was the only person who ever called him 'Michael') "you've been in the choir all this time, and I had no idea that you had such a voice!"

"That…that was absolutely wonderful!" gushed Mrs. Palmer. "Why, I'll bet you could sing the solo for Sunday's service!" All the kids began whispering and giggling again at this. So, Mike got his laugh, but not the way he expected. He didn't know until that moment that he really could sing and wasn't quite sure what to make of it.

On the way home from choir practice, Danny asked him a thousand questions but Joey teased him endlessly, calling him "Mike the Magnificent" and saying "That…that was wonderful" in a falsetto voice.

"You better quit it before I knock your face in," growled Mike. He would have too, but they were in front of the Edwards' house, and Joey escaped inside before Mike could get him. When Mike got to his house, he found his mom just home from work and starting dinner as he came in.

"Mom! Everybody says I can sing, even Mrs. Roberts and Mrs. Palmer."

"Yes, honey," she replied, without looking up. "Of course, you can."

"But, Mom, I mean for real. They gave me a solo and said maybe I could even sing it in church next Sunday!"

"Oh, Mike," said Meg, smiling and putting an arm around him. "That's excellent. See, Pastor Dave was right. God does have good things in store for you."

* * * * * *

"Now isn't that special," Awmal muttered. He didn't even notice Nawgaf standing beside him until he felt a rough shove.

"I beg your pardon," said his superior in a nasty tone. "What was that you said?"

"I *said,*" retorted Awmal, angry at the shove, "what's so special? Is he the only human that can sing?"

"Do you think I would be interested if this were *just* about his singing?"

"And just why are you so interested in him?" asked Awmal impatiently. "It's been almost twelve years, and you've never told me the whole story." Nawgaf turned to face Awmal with a condescending look and mock patience in his voice.

"Surely, you know that human beings are born with a number of talents and abilities. If you care to notice, this *particular* human being seems to have quite a few. He is a leader. He has brains and courage, though he doesn't know it yet. He even can sing. His destiny, and I get this from sources near the very top, is to be a man of great influence. And thanks to *your* incompetence HE IS ABOUT TO GIVE IT ALL TO THAT OTHER CAUSE!!!" Nawgaf struggled to control himself. "Do you in that minuscule mind of yours have any idea of the number of other human beings this one can influence for HIM if he continues on at this rate? Do you? DO YOU?!" Awmal, now shaken by this outburst knew quite well that the "Him" Nawgaf was referring to was the Great Holy One whose name neither of them dared mention.

    "Alright" he said diplomatically, "what can we do about it? The boy's angel is strong. There are people who pray to the Holy One on his behalf. Worse of all, even his parents are now more interested in the other side. What do you expect me to do?"

Nawgaf folded his arms and looked into the distance.

    "We must use our oldest and surest method. The boy can sing - let him. Encourage it. He wants to be noticed, let him be so especially by the one in whom he's developed his little "interest." Let the others give him all the attention for his talents that he desires. And when in his own heart these become more important than the Holy One and his cause," Nawgaf 's snout twisted up into a sneer *"then we'll have him!"*

Chapter 9

Mike's Dilemma

"You were really good on Sunday."

The voice made Mike's head jerk up from the library computer screen, and suddenly he was looking up into Venetia's gorgeous gray green eyes. They were a wonderful contrast to the gray skies that rainy Tuesday afternoon.

"What are you doing here?" she said smiling. "You have a computer at home, don't you?" Mike felt a bit of shyness come over him, and he shrugged a bit and looked down at the keyboard.

"My dad's using it because he's working at home today. I wanted to surf the net so my mom said to come here." Mike glanced back up again. It seemed the more he looked at Venetia, the prettier she got. "You were there? I mean, at church on Sunday?"

"I sure was," returned Venetia. "Remember, I'm spending part of the summer with my grandmother, and this week she made me come to church with her. I didn't know you could sing like that!"

Mike tried to appear cool in response to the compliment, but he couldn't help smiling even a little. He'd already gotten more compliments than he could count after he sang for this Sunday's service. His mom and dad, Pastor Dave, even people he didn't know. But this compliment was special. It was after all Venetia, super popular Venetia, to hear Joey tell it. The library was quiet, and there weren't a lot of people around that day. She was still smiling at him, and suddenly, he felt very comfortable, comfortable enough to ask her a question.

"Joey said that Danny's mom and your mom were talking, and that you're in another religion, and you don't really go to church."

"Well, that's true, kinda," said Venetia, now leaning forward a bit and lowering her voice since one of the librarians was looking at them for talking too loudly. "I mean, we don't go to a church, but we kind of make our own church, like our own space."

"Your own space?" echoed Mike.

"Yeah, like in my room, I have a special shelf, where I keep stuff that's important to me. And then I make a circle, and once I make it and go inside it, it's my special space to like pray and talk to the god and goddess."

"God and goddess?" said Mike surprised. "I thought God was a 'he'."

"Only 'cause that's what they tell you," said Venetia with a giggle. "When I was little, and we used to go to Mass, they said God was Father, Son and Holy Spirit, all male. But now, since we've been with our group, we see god as being both male and female."

"And you always do it all by yourself?" asked Mike.

"Not always," replied Venetia. "Sometimes our group gets together, especially on special days, like Halloween." ✳ witch??.

"Do you have a minister or somebody that teaches you and stuff?"

"Sort of, but the main thing about it and what's different than your church and all is that nobody tries to tell you what you're supposed to do and not do. Each person is free to talk to the god and goddess and the spirits and serve Mother Earth however they want, as long as we don't hurt anybody or do anything bad."

"But," pressed Mike, "how do you know what's bad if nobody teaches you anything?"

"I didn't say that nobody ever teaches anything," said Venetia, giggling again.

"There is a lot more than what I'm telling you though. Wait, move over; I'll show you." With a few clicks of the mouse, Venetia had cleared Mike's search and brought up on the screen a whole list of sites that had to do with what she was talking about. She clicked onto a few, some were question and answer, and others seemed to be general information.

"I'm not about to sit here and try to tell you what religion you should be," Venetia said pointedly, "but if you ever want to learn more about mine, a lot's here and in books too."

 Mike was intrigued by what Venetia was telling him, yet somehow, something seemed to trouble him very deeply, and he wasn't sure why. But of all the guys in the world, Sunnie's super pretty big sister was in the library, sitting on the same seat with him and talking to him. Not Joey, not even one of the older guys but him. And troubled as he was, he didn't want her to stop. "First, there was Sunday, and now this," Mike thought to himself, leaning back a bit and shoving his hands into his pockets, just as she was finishing her last sentence. His right hand hit a piece of paper, and he pulled it out.

Mike's Dilemma

Mike's jeans had been through the wash, so the paper was dry and brittle, but still readable. It was the instructions to the Ouija board that they had played with weeks ago on Memorial Day.

"That's weird," he thought out loud. Mike wondered if it would keep Venetia talking to him a little bit longer.

"Do they do this in your religion?" he said, handing her the paper.

"If they want to," replied Venetia. "Here, look." With a few more clicks, Mike was shocked to see right there on the computer screen the letters, the numbers, the "yes – no" almost exactly like the one Joey pulled out of the bag. And what was really weird was that instead of a planchette, a little tear drop shape floated eerily across the screen.

"I've done this a million times" Venetia was saying. "Hey, you want to ask it something?"

It seemed to Mike that every warning that his mom, Danny's mom, and Pastor Dave had given them tumbled into his mind all at once. But he didn't want Venetia to think he was scared or not cool. Mike just started to open his mouth when Venetia's cell phone rang. She answered it quickly under the glaring eyes of the librarian. Mike used the distraction to slip his hand over the mouse and exit the site.

"Hello? Not much, I'm at the library. Yeah, nothing else much to do. I'll meet you there, I'm leaving now." Venetia put a hand on Mike's shoulder as she stood up. "I gotta go; that was my boyfriend," she said with her trademark giggle. "But remember," she said over her shoulder, "if you're really interested in this stuff, we can talk some more.

"Wait," said Mike. "Youth meetings at church for the summer are on Wednesday after lunch and Friday nights. You and Sunnie wanna come?"

"I don't know. Sunnie might want to. Maybe it would be fun to see what you guys do. See ya." And with that, she disappeared around a corner.

Mike's Dilemma

Chapter 10

Mike's Dilemma

"What are you doing here? I thought you were staying downtown with your mom," Mike said, surprised to see Sunnie Powers playing with a small dog in her grandmother's front yard. It was Wednesday afternoon in early August, just about a week after Mike's library meeting with Sunnie's older sister Venetia. The Wednesday afternoon youth session at the church had just ended. Mike announced that he was going for a burger, and it seemed that everyone wanted to go with him - Joey, Danny, Kate, Corrie, and Reggie - the whole gang. Mike had been walking at the head of the group, half singing and half telling them about a new song he heard on the radio. Danny chimed in that his mom just bought a new gospel CD with that same song that Mike was singing. Kate was sure that their choir would never learn a song like that because Mrs. Roberts would never be able to play it on the piano.

"Sing it again Mike," Corrie said. "Maybe we can learn it anyway - from you." Mike was just about to happily grant that request when he looked up and saw Sunnie in Mrs. Power's front yard. Sunnie picked up the dog and opened the gate to let everyone in.

"Venetia wanted to go back home, so I came here again," she replied in answer to Mike's question.

"Why?" asked Joey. "Doesn't she like it here?" Sunnie shook her head.

"She says it's boring out here, and my grandmother doesn't let her boyfriend come over like my mom does. Besides," Sunnie's face darkened a bit, "I like it better here than at home when all her friends come over. She thinks you're pretty cool though," Sunnie added, looking at Mike. "You and Joey. She said she saw you at the library." Mike shrugged.

"She came in while I was on the Net. She showed me some stuff on the computer, that's all." Mike quickly changed the subject before anyone could ask just what it was that she showed him. "Come on, everybody, let's go get those burgers; I'll sing the rest of the song on the way. Are you coming, Sunnie?" Sunnie went to put the dog inside and get her grandmother's permission, and soon the whole group was on their way.

Mike absolutely savored the whole time. Ever since he sang at church it seemed that all his friends were hanging on his every word, especially when he was singing. And Mike was doing that as much as possible even in the shower and on the street. Once a couple of people even stopped when they heard him and said, "Wow, you have a really nice voice" and he never even saw them before! And this day as they munched their burgers and fries by the large pane glass window at the local McDonalds, all the kids were paying attention to him as he showed them the new song and a few others besides. Even Joey listened without interrupting. So Mike wasn't a little sorry when Corrie announced that it was time that she and Kate got going. They and Reggie Matthews had just gone, and Sunnie was throwing away her trash when Mike saw a huge black SUV zoom into the parking lot; it looked like the same one that splashed them with water that Friday before Memorial Day.

"Mike, look," said Joey, just as Venetia and a tall kid, dressed in black jeans and a black tee shirt with a silk-screened skull on it, jumped out. Mike was now speechless, as Venetia glided over in her usual breezy way and with her usual gorgeous smile, her tall friend close behind. She had something in clear plastic over one arm, while the other reached back for the guy.

"I called Grandma and she said you'd be here. Seems you forgot your dress for Sunday, so we brought it up," she said, while handing Sunnie the dress. "Guys" she continued, "this is my boyfriend Cal McKay. Cal, this is Mike, who I was telling you about. Joey, you already know, and I know you've seen Danny around too."

"Hey," said Cal, looking at each of them in turn under half-closed eyelids. Joey grinned and said "hey" back, but Mike stared at Cal. Spiky red-dyed hair, tattoos on both arms, and lots of body piercing: both ears, lower lip, even his tongue. Mike wondered if he would have to look like Cal to get a girl like Venetia to like him.

"Joey, Mike," said Danny in an urgent whisper "we have to go too." "Oh, hey," said Venetia. "Sunnie, why don't you take your dress back to Grandma's and Danny you can walk with her. Joey and Mike can catch up later. Me and Cal want to ask them something. With that she slid herself into the seat right across from Mike and Cal sat down next to her. Sunnie shrugged and headed towards the door, but Danny hesitated.

"Go," said Joey. "We're coming in a minute."

"OK," said Venetia after watching Danny and Sunnie go out the door. "The last time I was at your church with my grandmother I heard somebody say that you guys were helping out at the old house that belongs to that young preacher's father; is that true?"

"Well, yeah," said Mike. "It's the old Palmer Mansion. But Danny works with us too. You don't want him to know what you're gonna ask us?" Venetia and Cal exchanged glances.

"Lets just say that with him being younger and all, he may not be mature enough to know," said Venetia with a smile. "Not like you guys."

"You mean you don't want him to tell his mom," said Joey, snickering. "Yeah, something like that. And I don't want Sunnie telling my grandmother either. This is just between us. OK?"

Joey shrugged and nodded. Mike felt uneasy, but he didn't want to be out of the loop. So he nodded too. Venetia continued, leaning forward for emphasis.

"This is the thing. Mike, remember when we were in the library and I was telling you about my religion, and how we sometimes meet in groups? Well, Cal and some of the other guys in our group think that the Palmer house would be a really cool place to have one of our meetings."

"Why?" asked Mike.

"'Cause of all the stuff that's happened there," said Cal. "Like, isn't it true that they were really rich and stuff, and that there was money in the house, and a couple of people died in there?"

"Died?" said Joey now exited. "Heck, somebody was murdered there; that's what I heard. And there's still a lot of neat stuff in the basement, old armor and everything."

"Wow," said Venetia giggling. "Way cool. I bet in a place like that, a place with history I mean, it would be really easy for us to get in touch with our spirit guides."

"Spirit guides?" said Mike.

"Yeah, sure," said Cal. "We could go in, have our gig, and you know, kinda look around some."

"You mean outside in the yard?" asked Mike.

"I mean whatever. You know, it wouldn't make sense for us to come all the way out here to meet and not see anything," replied Cal with a half grin. "Venetia told me that Danny's mom said you guys actually got into the basement. And my best friend Rick, he says he's seen you guys around there too. If you guys kinda help us out getting in and all, I mean like we'd really appreciate it. And remember, you guys are gonna be in junior high downtown this year. If you're in good with us guys in high school, it could help you out a lot," he added slowly nodding, still looking at them through half closed eyes.

"Sure, we'll help," replied Joey "Right, Mike?"

Mike looked down at the table top for a moment, then up at Venetia.

"Oh, come on," said Venetia. "It's just for a couple of hours on one night. The yard is so big no one will know we were there. We'll have our meeting and then leave. Right, Cal?"

"Yeah, sure," Cal said, grinning his half grin again.

"I don't know," said Mike looking down again. "I guess. Your friend Rick-is his last name Jeffries?"

"Yeah," said Cal still half grinning. "He says he knows you guys real well."

"It's all settled then," said Venetia. She jumped up from her seat, pulling Cal up with her. "We have to plan everything so we'll let you know just when. See ya later!" They headed out, and Venetia smiled over her shoulder, waving at them with her fingers. Cal didn't look back at all, as the two of them disappeared through the glass doors.

Chapter 11

Mike's Dilemma

A week from that next Saturday at just about 11 AM, Mike took his place behind the microphone and stood up as straight and tall as he could. His freshly dry cleaned suit felt a little stiff, and his tie felt a bit tight, but he took a deep breath, clasped his hands in front and put his shoulders back just like Mrs. Roberts had instructed him. She pounded out the first chords of the introduction and everyone at the Community Fellowship Church's Annual Ladies Brunch smiled with anticipation at their very special guest Michael Bryant. ("And you'd better make a good job of it," Pastor Dave said the evening before with a chuckle "since I'm letting you out of youth service to rehearse!") Mike was a little nervous at first, but that melted away as he belted out the verses to "Onward Christian Solders." He was careful to keep eye contact with his audience and barely even looked at his 'cheat sheet' that was carefully folded in his left hand. His mom was absolutely beaming, and even Mike Senior consented to suffer through the program in order to hear his son perform. By the time he was done, Mike practically expected the standing ovation that his appreciative audience gave him before he ran home to get out of that suit and tie.

"Weren't you even scared?" Corrie Thompson asked him as a bunch of kids stood on the church steps handing out flyers after the brunch was over. Mike had changed and came back to help hand out the notices for Friday night's skating party, which would be the last big event of the summer

Youth program.

"Nope," replied Mike, who was still basking in the glow of his performance. Even now, grownups leaving the brunch were still congratulating him with words like "Great job" and "Wonderful voice" and "Keep up the good work." Mike felt so on top of the world that he almost passed by his mom who stopped to give him another hug and say "Don't stay out too late" before she headed home, and his dad went to the office to get some weekend work done.

"Come on," said Joey. "You had to be a little bit scared."

"I swear I wasn't," boasted Mike. He handed out his last flyer and came back to sit on the church steps with the others. "Look, I read the words over and over, and then I practiced it until I got it right. That was it; why would I be scared?"

"Well," said Corrie, "you really do sing well and you did a great job today." Everyone nodded in agreement, and Mike was just opening his mouth to talk some more about himself, his singing, and his bravery when the now familiar black SUV roared around the corner and screeched to a stop at the curb in front of them. The passenger side door swung open, and Rick stuck his head out the door, and Cal leaned over from the driver's side.

"Yo, what's up?" called Rick. "Why don't you two get in?" Joey jumped off the church steps and trotted towards the curb. Mike suddenly felt strangely sick to his stomach, and for a couple of seconds, he couldn't even move. He could actually feel everyone staring at him.

"You're gonna go with *them?*" Reggie asked .

"What's the matter?" called Joey from the back seat. "You *scared* or something?"

Mike looked around quickly, his previous bravado turning to a vague feeling of dread.

"No, I'm not scared, I'm coming." Rick jumped out of the front seat and climbed into the back with Joey.

"You know more about where we're going than I do," he said with half a grin.

Mike could hear a "Wow" over his shoulder as he was getting in, but he didn't bother to turn and see which of the kids had said it. And he didn't bother to ask where they were going: he knew. From the top of his head to the tips of his toenails, Mike knew that this was wrong. Still, in a way it felt good to be hanging out with Cal and being picked up in the coolest SUV around. Even Rick didn't seem so bad now, giving him the front seat in front of everybody.

"So what's the best way to get in there," Cal said while pulling off. "And we need something around the back like, so the whole world doesn't see us when we go in."

"Go straight down here, and make a left at the light," said Mike after a deep breath. "Then keep straight down Hathaway Avenue. I'll let you know where to turn next."

* * * * * *

Mike's Dilemma

Shamael and Jediael floated above the SUV as it threaded its way through the quiet suburban streets.

"Cockamamie plan number two, I see," grumbled Jediael. "I thought those two had learned their lesson."

"How many humans do you know that learned their lesson the first time?" replied Shamael. "Still, this is definitely not good, and there's not a thing we can do about it but be here."

"Free will is free will, huh?"

"That's how the Holy One designed it. He didn't create any of us to be puppets, my friend; and our two guys have definitely chosen to do what they are about to do."

The angels spent the next half hour watching Mike and Joey show Cal and Rick the quickest way onto the Palmer property. Mike even showed them the back entrance, just across from the heavily wooded strip of land that separated the property from the main street behind. The older teenagers got out of the SUV, walked around a bit, peered through the fence at the side and back of the house and gardens, which were in various stages of repair.

"You think we can do it?" asked Rick, when they jumped back into the SUV.

"I know we can," replied Cal with a snort. "It'll be easier than I thought. Hey, you two," he said over his shoulder to Joey and Mike, who were by now both in the back seat. "We're gonna go to my house cause everybody's there, and it's only a few minutes from Hathaway. I'll drop you home in about an hour."

The McKay house was crawling with demons. Shamael and Jediael stood quietly and generally unnoticed by the busy evil spirits, while they watched Mike and Joey follow Cal and Rick through the back door and down the steps into the basement The latest rock CD screamed from the stereo out into the well manicured streets of the fashionable neighborhood at the edge of town. Mike looked uncomfortable until he saw Venetia in the middle of the floor. She was laughing and talking with several teenagers that Mike had never seen before. Joey pointed out several that he knew because they also lived near Danny. Even Sunnie was there, sitting in a corner scowling, arms folded across her chest. A tall stern faced angel stood near her, and both Shamael and Jediael silently nodded their greetings, which he returned.

"He looks about as grim as I feel in this place," said Jediael, referring to their colleague. Shamael was sure Awmal and Nawgaf were somewhere nearby, but there were so many evil spirits in the place, it was hard to tell. He could see several around the large and well-stocked bar, and one was standing guard over a card table that held a Ouija board and a stack of Tarot cards. The rest were slithering along the polished wooden floor under the upholstered chairs . One even stood over Rick, who had quickly found a spot in the corner next to Angie, his girlfriend. They were necking hot and heavy when Cal leaned over them.

"Hey, you two," he said laughing. "There are kids in here. Do that upstairs someplace, like the den."

"You heard the man," said Rick. "He said we can do this in private."

Angie hesitated. "What if someone up there sees us?"

"Nobody's home," replied Cal. My dad's gone on business, and our maid has the day off."

"What if your mom comes home?" said Angie, still not sure.

"My mom hasn't come home for five years," said Cal, laughing again.

* * * * * *

Rick pulled Angie by the arm and they headed up to the den. Meantime, Mike slipped over to the opposite corner, where Sunnie was sitting.

"What are you doing here? I thought you'd be at your grandma's," said Mike.

"She had to go away for the weekend, so I had to go home. And now, my mom's having some special meeting with her friends, and she said I had to go with Venetia. Why are you with Cal?" Mike shrugged.

"He saw me and Joey, and he gave us a ride in the SUV," he replied, carefully leaving out the part about the Palmer place. Mike paused a second, not even sure himself why he would ask. "Does the special meeting have to do with your religion?"

"Yeah," returned Sunnie "but I don't know what, and I don't care. I hate it; I'd much rather go to church with my grandmother."

"Why?" asked Mike. "What's there to hate?"

"Well," said Sunnie, leaning over and lowering her voice, "my grandma says it's evil, even though my mom says it isn't. Venetia likes it, especially because Cal is in it too. I can't stand him; he's always drinking beer, and he's always making fun of me."

"Hey, Mike, come here," interrupted Joey before Mike could respond. "Venetia says she's gonna show us something."

"Over here, guys" called Venetia. "Mike, I wanted to show you the Ouija board again since I didn't get a chance at the library. Cal, sit with me; let's do it together."

Cal sauntered over and slid into the seat opposite Venetia, and they both rested their fingers on the planchette in the middle of the board.

Venetia closed her eyes, as if she were concentrating.

"Spirit in the Ouija board… um…should we have our meeting in the yard at the Palmer house?"

Everyone stopped to watch. At first nothing, but then slowly Cal and Venetia's hands began to move as the planchette slid slowly and steadily, stopping over the "yes" at the bottom of the board.

"Come on- you guys are pushing it," said one of the teenagers.

"We are not," said Venetia. "It really does work. I'll ask it something else. Ouija board, when should we have our meeting?" Another eternity seemed to pass, but then the planchette started moving again. Joey stared transfixed, but Mike felt as though icy fingers were walking down his spine.

The planchette stopped towards the beginning of the alphabet.

"A B C D …F," said another of the teenagers. "Maybe F for Friday?"

"Friday?" said Joey, "that's when the big skating party is gonna be for the Youth Program at church."

"That's perfect," squealed Venetia. Cal looked up blankly. "Don't you see?" she whispered. "Nobody will be there; they'll all be at the roller rink. Come on," she said smiling. "Let's ask it one more thing. Ouija board, Cal and me will be together forever and ever, right?" Everyone waited, but nothing else happened.

"Must be bad vibes," said Cal, standing up. "Anybody else want a beer?" Cal went over to the refrigerator behind the bar, and everyone else except Venetia, Mike, Joey, and Sunnie moved back to their seats or over to the bar to help themselves from the case he was pulling from the fridge. Mike spoke up.

"If you and Cal didn't move it," he said to Venetia "how do you know it wasn't an evil spirit, like a demon or something?"

"Because the Ouija board isn't an evil spirit," she replied. People always say that our religion deals with evil spirits, and Satan and stuff, but that's not true. Our spirits aren't evil; most of them are there to help us. I mean, some people are into the bad stuff, but we're not. We only deal with good spirits, like our spirit guides. And, besides, the board gave a good answer. If we go Friday, nobody will bother us and we can't bother anybody 'cause they won't be there, right?" Mike wasn't sure that Venetia's logic made much sense to him, but before he could say anything, he heard the snap of a flip top can.

"Hey, you guys ever had a beer before?" Cal said grinning, and extending the can towards them.

"No! And I don't want any from you," retorted Sunnie. But Joey just shrugged.

"I have. My dad let me taste it a couple of times." Joey took the can and put it to his lips and took several big gulps. He laughed a little, wiping his mouth with the back of one hand and giving the can back to Cal with the other.

"What about you, Mike?" said Cal. "You gonna be a chicken baby like Sunnie?"

"I AM NOT!" Sunnie snapped back. Cal just laughed and stuck the can under Mike's nose. Mike looked at Joey, but he only stared back at him with a peculiar half smile. Venetia was looking at him too.

"Come on, Mike. Don't be scared." she cajoled. "Everybody has a first time."

Mike took deep breath. *Dad would probably shoot me for this,* he thought. But he felt dumb with everybody looking at him, and he didn't want to look chicken.

"I'm not scared." Mike reached for the can and took a tiny sip. It was the nastiest thing he ever tasted, worse than spinach. He handed it back quickly, resisting the temptation to spit it out.

"See," said Venetia to Sunnie. "Mike tasted it, how come you're being such a baby?"

Sunnie looked back defiantly, took the can and sipped.

"It's awful!" she said making a face. "How can you drink this stuff?" Venetia shrugged.

"You get used to it. Besides," she added with a giggle, "you don't drink it just for the taste."

"Yeah," shot back Sunnie, "you just drink it 'cause your boyfriend likes it."

"And you're just jealous 'cause you wish you had a boyfriend and you don't." Venetia gave Sunnie a quick shove, making her fall right into Joey, so that they both fell backwards. Joey burst into laughter, letting himself fall on the floor. Sunnie jumped up quickly. Hurt and embarrassment covered her face, and her eyes began to fill with tears.

"I hate you!" she yelled at Venetia and ran up the stairs.

"Don't go into the den," called Cal. "It's occupied."

"What's wrong with her?" said someone else.

"Forget it," said Venetia. "She's always minding my business, trying to get me into trouble. I say one thing about her, and her feelings get hurt. Let her run upstairs and cry."

Mike was dumbfounded, but as he looked at Joey on the floor, still giggling after his 'taste' of beer, it slowly began to dawn on him why Sunnie was so upset. Why would Venetia be so mean? He looked up at Cal. "It's been an hour," he said, "and me and Joey really have to get home."

"Sure, kid," replied Cal. Mike said he would wait upstairs, but he really wanted to look for Sunnie. He found her not far from the top of the basement stairs near the back door.

"I didn't know you liked Joey," he said softly.

"So?" shot back Sunnie wiping her eyes. "What difference does it make? He doesn't like me back." Mike looked down and shuffled his feet a bit.

"Did he ever say he didn't like you? I mean how do you know?"

"He doesn't talk to me; you talk to me more than he does," replied Sunnie. "Venetia said if I liked him so much, I should make a circle and cast a spell to get him to like me. But, like I said, my grandmother said that stuff was evil and I told Venetia that she said so. That's why she was making fun of me in front of Joey, Cal, and everybody. Sometimes I just can't stand her." It all seemed really strange to Mike. Sunnie was smart, pretty, and the most popular kid in their class. He would never have imagined her crying because her sister had trashed her, and over Joey, of all people.

"Well," he said, "maybe Joey will like you without the spell." They both turned and looked towards the basement door. Venetia was coming up the steps with Cal close behind, pulling along a stumbling and still loudly laughing Joey. "Besides," added Mike, "I have a feeling Joey won't even remember what happened."

* * * * * *

"That's probably true," murmured Jediael to Shamael, as the two hovered above while Venetia and Cal climbed into the front seats of Cal's SUV. Joey sat between Mike and Sunnie in the back and almost immediately fell asleep. "He may sleep now," continued Jediael, "but I don't think he'll like how he feels when he wakes up. And I don't like where this is going; I really don't."

"Neither do I, but…" Before Shamael could say anything else, the two angels were suddenly pushed apart, and Nawgaf appeared between them. Awmal hung close behind.

"Don't bother," snarled Nawgaf, when Shamael and Jediael reached for their swords. "I'm not here to fight you. Not that I would have fought you two over them anyway. I think our plan is working very nicely, don't you Awmal?" Still mindful of the angel's swords, Awmal stayed behind Nawgaf, but let out a nasty snicker all the same. Nawgaf focused a yellow eye on Jediael. "That's especially true for the one that belongs to you. But don't worry" he added looking at Shamael. "The other will be coming our way also. Just you wait and see!" The two sped off, their laughter trailing in the distance. The two angels watched them go and then silently rose to follow the SUV as it pulled away from the curb.

"You know," said Jediael, "our guys won't be kids for much longer. Soon they'll be teenagers, and who's to say that we won't get other assignments? Especially if they don't…"

"Don't lose hope," said Shamael. "Remember what Magdiel said.

The Holy One will always work things together for the good of those who love Him. He loves our guys, and some of those who love Him love our guys too. And they're still praying."

Mike's Dilemma

Chapter 12

Mike's Dilemma

The grandfather clock in the living room had just struck four o'clock when Mike slipped inside the side door and passed his mom, who was just starting dinner.

"You're home early," she said, but was interrupted by the phone ringing. Mike had already started upstairs when she hung up.

"Mike, come here please," she called.

"Yeah, Mom?"

"That was Mrs. Roberts. She called to say that someone at church saw you and another boy get into a car with Cal McKay in front of the church this afternoon."

"Mom! That was Joey," said Mike. "Cal gave us a ride in his SUV."

"A ride? A ride to where?"

"Well," said Mike cautiously "Cal drove by Pastor Dave's house, and then he took us to his house."

"His house? What in the name of heaven were you doing there?" Mike's mom saw to it that the discussion continued over dinner after his dad had come home.

"Mike, you know how I feel about you riding in cars and going places with people when I don't know about it," she said between bites. "Cal McKay is much older than you and Joey, and I want to be able to talk to the parent of anybody whose house you go to."

Mike's Dilemma

Mike Sr. was more diplomatic.

"Meg, it's not as if we don't know the man. Greg Edwards has been John McKay's right hand man at McKay Industries for years, and I've done plenty of consulting work for him myself. And both we and the Edwards were at his Christmas party last year." Mike Sr. sighed. "The boy invited them for a ride and they went. Boys do these things, no harm done. Even so, Mike, your mother is right. You shouldn't go places without one of us knowing where. Besides, what were you doing at Cal's house?"

"Well, there were lots of kids there," Mike began. "We listened to music, and we were talking, and…"

"Was there any smoking or drinking in there?" demanded Meg. Mike felt like his heart fell into his shoes. Of all things, why on earth did she have to ask *that*? Mike looked down at his lap.

"There was some beer there," he murmured.

"BEER?" shouted Meg. "You were in that man's house drinking *beer*?"

"But, Mom!" cried Mike "I only took a tiny sip! Everybody was drinking it. Even Sunnie took a sip. It was Joey that tried to drink the whole can!" Meg turned her sternest glare on Mike Sr.

"And you say there's no harm done?" Mike Sr. held up his hand.

"OK, OK. Mike, I admit that I never took the time to have this discussion with you before. That was my fault, and so I can't really punish you this first time. But you must realize that drinking any kind of alcohol, even a little sip, is totally off limits for you."

"But, Dad, everybody was drinking it. If I didn't I would've looked chicken."

"And so what?" replied his dad. "Isn't it better to stand alone and do what is right than to follow the crowd when they are wrong? Drinking alcohol is something even adults have to be very careful about, and it is definitely something that someone your age ought to avoid altogether, no matter what everybody else does. Do you understand me?"

"Yes, sir," said Mike, looking down again. They ate in silence for a few minutes, until Mike spoke up again.

"Mom, is it evil to cast a spell on somebody?" Meg put her fork down and looked at Mike.

"Why would you ask?"

"Somebody told me that you could put a spell on somebody, but that it was evil." replied Mike. He thought it best to leave out the names.

"Well, back home, some people try to do things like that, maybe cut up a bird and sprinkle the blood or go to the 'wise woman' in the village to mix a potion or something like that. But your grand mommy always taught me that such things didn't really work; and if they seemed to, it was really the work of Satan. And yes, it would be wrong to do it." Mike looked at his dad.

"Down south where I grew up," he said between bites, "some folk did stuff like "work roots," or try to put a 'hex' on somebody, but Big Momma would have punished us for sure if we even talked about doing anything like that. She said, 'If you need something, then you pray to God and ask him for it.' Like your mom's people, my grand mamma said stuff like that was wicked because it went against the word of God."

Mike was quiet a moment before he looked up again.

"How come you guys don't go to church anymore like you did when you were kids? I don't mean sometimes but all the time, like Danny's mom?"

"Oh, I don't know, son," said Mike Sr. "Seems like there's so much work to do, just never can find the time I guess."

"But I think it's time for a change," said Meg, looking at both her Mikes, junior and senior. "The more I think about it, the more I think we need to start making the time. Starting this very Sunday."

Mike's parents were as good as their word, and sure enough, the next morning the Bryant family was up, dressed, and walking towards Community Fellowship Church. When the three of then got to the Edwards' house, Mike ran up and rang the bell. Danny came bounding out the door, and when Nina Edwards saw that both Mr. and Mrs. Bryant were going, she called out to them to wait a moment, and soon Teddy was hustled out the door to the sidewalk.

"Do you mind taking Teddy too?" she asked. "I'd never be able to make it today, and, besides, Joey was up half the night with a headache, and he's still in bed now." Ms. Meg looked at Mike Sr. and then back at Ms. Nina.

"Well, you do know about yesterday when the kids were at the McKay's house - don't you?"

"Oh yes, I know," said Nina. But as Greg says, 'Boys will be boys.' And you know how close Greg is with Mr. McKay," she added with a little laugh. "I guess Joey was just trying to impress Cal." Mike's mom was about to say something else, but his dad interrupted with "We'll be glad to bring Teddy along" and soon the five of them were on their way.

"You remember about the big skating party this Friday, right?" Mike said to Danny as they walked.

"Oh, I don't know if I'm going to be there."

"No?" said Meg. "That's too bad, why not?"

"Well," said Danny, "first, next weekend is our weekend to stay with our mom. Second, Mom has to work Friday and Saturday night so my grandmother is coming to visit."

"That's right," put in Meg. "I'll be working with your mom on Friday night."

"Yeah," continued Danny. "And it's gonna be Teddy's birthday, and Mom wants me to help with the party."

"I'm gonna be five years old," piped in Teddy. "There's gonna be a clown and cotton candy and everything!"

"Besides," added Danny, "my mom said that if the party is over soon enough, maybe grandma could still take us later."

Soon they arrived at church; Mike's mom picked seats right near the front. Pastor Dave preached the sermon that day, and this time Mike actually thought he understood almost every thing that was said.

"God is our refuge and our strength," he said. "He is a 'very present help in times of trouble.' That means any kind of trouble that we're in: at work, or school, with our families - anything. He may not answer our prayers the way we think He should, but if we are in Christ, He is there to help us in the way He knows best."

When the invitation was given, Mike's mom took his hand and looked at Mike Sr. They all stood up and went with the others who were going forward. Even Teddy and Danny got up and followed, even though they both had prayed and given their hearts to Jesus before. Mike even noticed Sunnie coming too, holding her grandmother's hand. Soon, everyone was kneeling at the altar and Pastor Roberts led them all in a prayer. They admitted they were sinners, and they knew that Jesus shed his blood for them. Then they asked God to forgive them for their sins and asked Jesus to come and live in them and fill them with his Spirit. Mike closed his eyes tight when he prayed the prayer and meant every word. Afterwards, he was surprised how good he felt - like cleaner than he ever felt before, but on the inside. After church, Mike thought that Pastor Dave would shake his hand right off. And Mrs. Roberts not only gave Mike a big hug, but she took him to the church office, reached into a box and gave Mike his very own copy of the Bible, not a kiddy one, like he had at home, but a real Bible with neat pictures and everything. Mike felt so different that he even sneaked into the boys' room during fellowship hour to look in the mirror to see if he looked any different. Of course he didn't, but almost as soon as he looked at himself, his conscience began to bother him. "You told Mom and Dad about the beer, but you didn't tell them the whole truth about that ride with Cal and Rick," his image seemed to say. "What's the big deal; they're only going in the yard for a little while," Mike argued back to himself. "Joey's my friend, and Cal and Venetia want to be my friends too. Even Rick was nice to us yesterday. If I say something, I'll look like a chicken and a traitor and we're all in trouble." Yet try as he might, Mike couldn't shake the thought. Should he say anything or not?

Mike's Dilemma

Chapter 13

Mike's Dilemma

Mike was still arguing with himself, even right up until the big skating party the following Friday night. And the place was packed. Everybody was there - Pastor and Mrs. Roberts, Pastor Dave and his wife April, the whole church staff. Practically everyone in the congregation showed up- even if they couldn't skate -just to be at the party. Even people from other churches came. Mike's mom dropped him off at the rink on her way to work the overnight shift at the hospital.

"It's just going on seven o'clock," she said. "You can stay until the party is over at eleven, but be sure to call your dad in time to come and pick you up. And let the phone ring, because he's going to try to get in some extra sleep while the house is quiet."

Mike worked his way through the knots of people standing around the door of the rink chatting and drinking homemade punch. The security guy on the door (one of the church's ushers) took his ticket and stamped his hand. Mike traded his sneakers for skates at the rental window and eased his way into the crowded oval. An upbeat gospel song was blaring over the loudspeakers, and people of all shapes and sizes were skating, slipping and sliding their way around the rink.

Mike's Dilemma

"Hey, Mike," called Reggie. "Come skate with us." Mike made his way around to where Reg, Kate, and Corrie were feeling their way along the safety rail. He had just completed a circle when he felt a shove and then his arm being pulled by Joey, who was actually a better skater that all of them. He swung a beefy arm around Mike's shoulder and pushed him towards the center where the good skaters were and whispered in his ear.

"Remember, we go tonight!" Then as suddenly as he appeared, Joey pushed off and skating backwards, disappeared into the crowd. Mike stood still, startled for a moment. The thought that had been nagging him all week seemed to leave his mind and settle uneasily in the pit of his stomach.

"What should I do?" Mike said to himself. "If I don't go, then none of them will want to hang out with me anymore. Even Joey will probably want to hang with Cal more than me, and Venetia will think I'm immature, like Danny. And if I tell, they'll be so mad nobody will probably talk to me for a year! They're only going in the yard for an hour or so. It's not like before when we went inside." Yet despite all his arguments, Mike still felt bad about the whole thing, worse than when Venetia and Cal first asked him and Joey to help. The song finished, and another even faster song started, something about God being good. Mike's mind kept going back to Sunday, when he was kneeling in front of the church praying. Distracted, he moved into the middle layer of skaters, and slid along almost aimlessly until he bumped, literally, into Sunnie Powers.

"Sorry!" he called over the din, but it was as though she barely heard him. She waved and skated on. And so the hour passed. Fast music, slow music, couples only, a break for lemonade, skating with the other kids, skating alone. Oddly, he didn't see Joey again the whole time. He did see Sunnie again though, and someone else was bumping into her, but this time it was no accident. The guy was bigger than she was, and started pulling her by her arm.

"Hey, leave me alone!" yelled Sunnie. "I'm not going; I don't have to!" Mike was about to skate up, but he stopped short when he recognized that the guy was one of the kids at Cal's house the week before. And Rick Jeffries was close behind. He leaned over to whisper something to Sunnie, but she kept yelling.

"I said NO! I don't have to go now; my grandmother said I didn't." Almost immediately, several members of the security crew appeared. And so did Venetia. She didn't have on skates, and she ran across to where her sister was. Security hustled all of them off the skating floor to an area on the side. Mike didn't come off, but he slid over near the railing and stayed within earshot.

"It's OK; it's OK," Venetia said to the security guys. "This is my sister; she's with me. My mom is not home, and it's time for us to go. Sunnie, we have to go - now."

"I am not with you," retorted Sunnie. "Grandma said I could stay to the end."

"If you stay," said Venetia with a dirty look at Sunnie, "then we would have to come all the way back to get you. Cal doesn't want to do that." By now, Pastor Dave had come over to see what the ruckus was about.

"She can't make me," said Sunnie to Pastor Dave.

"Look, it's no big deal," said Venetia hurriedly. "We can drop you off at home." She started to pull Sunnie again, but Pastor Dave interrupted.

"If your grandmother said she could stay, what's the problem?" Venetia didn't answer Pastor Dave, she just put her hand on her hip and gave him a really dirty look up and down. He responded with a cool smile.

"We can solve this right now," he said, pulling his cell phone out of his pocket. "Sunnie, is your grandma home? What's her number?" Sunnie rattled off the numbers before Venetia could get out another word. Meanwhile, Mike noticed that Rick and the other guy slipped back into the crowd.

"Hello? Mrs. Powers? Pastor Dave here. Yes, fine, fine. It seems that Venetia... oh yes? I see. I understand. Right. Sure we can. No problem at all. You're very welcome, Mrs. Powers. See you at service on Sunday...yes, God bless you too." He turned back to Venetia. His lips were smiling, but his voice was ice cold.

"Your grandmother says that Sunnie has permission to stay here until the end and that she is supposed to stay at *her* house tonight, not home alone. You may leave if you like, but Sunnie stays here. I will see to it that she gets to your grandmother's. Understood?" Venetia still didn't answer a word; but flipping her hair over her shoulder, she turned and walked away, but not before making a rude gesture with her fingers. Before Mike could even digest what he saw, Joey was at his side again, sneakers on, and skates slung over his shoulder.

"Come on," he whispered in Mike's ear. "Now, while the security guys are still over here."

The warm evening air felt strange to Mike. But everything felt strange, even as he got back his shoes and followed Joey out the front door of the rink and around the back to where a knot of teens were standing together. Just about everyone who had come to the party was crowded inside, including the security guys, and the two of them had left the building without being noticed. It was just past eight thirty, and even though the mid-August dusk was soon to turn to twilight, he could make out the faces of Rick and three other kids who had been at Cal's. Venetia soon joined them.

"Where's Sunnie?" said the guy who had started to pull her out first. "Cal is gonna be really ticked off if he has to come back for her."

"Forget it; we don't have to come back for her," replied Venetia. "She's just gonna have to stay at my grandmother's. Hi, Mike. Hi, Joey," she added in her usual sweet singsong. Obviously, thought Mike, she didn't see him inside. "Come on, guys," continued Venetia. "We're gonna walk over and meet everybody else over at that 24 hour convenience store. Cal didn't want anybody to recognize his car over here." Mike hesitated and wandered over to the corner of the building, pretending that something caught his attention up the street towards the front, but then something really did catch his eye. A tiny red car pulled up to the curb, and not a moment passed before the door flew open and Danny jumped out, a roller skate in each hand with Teddy close behind. The birthday party must have been finished, and it seemed their grandma got them to the rink after all. Mike turned back to the others quickly. All he needed now was for Danny (or worse, Teddy) to see him and Joey and start asking a lot of questions. Hopefully, the huge size of the rink, and the dense crowd would be reason enough to Danny for not finding them.

"I know a shortcut from here," Rick was saying, setting out ahead. "We can pick up some beers at the store before we go." He laughed and punched the air with his fists. "It's gonna be hot tonight!" Soon everyone but Mike was laughing and talking about what they were going to do. Mike could hear Venetia go on about what a cool time they would have and what a neat place the Palmer yard would be. Even Joey was chattering about dead people in the house, buried money and the like, but Mike barely heard a word of it. All he could see in his mind's eye was what his mom's face would look like if she knew what he was doing right now. Not just anger, but disappointment, and lots of it. And he could hear his dad's voice too *"And so what? Isn't it better to stand alone and do what is right than to follow the crowd when they are wrong?"* The more Mike walked, the more he knew that he couldn't do this, he just couldn't. "But," he argued with himself, "what will they say if I don't go?" Suddenly the fifteen minute walk was over, and the group approached a long building with several store fronts. Most were shuttered tight, but the last one was lit up, and had a big yellow awning over the door. Large red letters advertised beer, lotto, soda, sandwiches, and "Open 24 Hours." Mike noticed the big black SUV parked out front with two or three other cars. The older kids all went inside, leaving Joey and Mike alone outside. Mike could see Rick joining Cal inside in front of the beer case. He knew what he had to do.

"Wanna go in?" asked Joey. "I got money for candy and stuff," he said, pulling two five dollar bills out of his pocket.

"I'm not going."

"Alright," replied Joey with a shrug. "I'll go in. What do you want?"

"I mean," said Mike, "I'm not going at all. We don't have any business doing this, Joey, and you know it. You know what happened the first time we went to the Palmer place. You heard what everybody said. So I'm not going. This is wrong, and I'm not gonna do it." Joey looked at him as if he had three heads or something.

"What the heck are you talking about? You promised you would come. You're the one always talking about how brave you are, and how you're never scared, and now you're gonna leave?" Suddenly, Rick came back outside.

"What's goin' on out here?" he demanded.

"It's him," said Joey, angrily throwing up his hands towards Mike. "Now, all of a sudden, he says he doesn't wanna go!"

"Nah, nah, man," said Rick, shaking his head. "It's too late, now you gotta come."

"Well, I'm not," replied Mike, but before the words were out, Rick's face contorted into an ugly grimace.

"Listen up, you little … What do you want to do? Run and tell your mommy on us or something?" Rick moved closer. He was already big, and the night shadows made him look even bigger in the dim light streaming from the store. "We got stuff goin' down tonight; and if you think you're gonna run now and tell, I'll put my fist right in your ugly…" Mike didn't wait to hear the end of the sentence, he spun around and bolted down the sidewalk just as Rick lunged at him.

"GET BACK HERE!" yelled Rick. He started to come after him, but Mike spied a trash can on the corner. He picked it up and hurled it back with all his might. Both Rick and Joey had to jump out of the way, giving Mike time to scramble around the corner. Mike started down the long sidewalk ahead of him with unfamiliar buildings and houses on either side. He looked around frantically for a place to hide. He slipped into the alley way behind the stores. He soon realized what the alley was used for, as he stumbled over mounds of big, shiny black garbage bags that glinted in the dim light of the street lamps above. Breathing hard, Mike ducked down between the full soft bags. A minute or so went by. Mike's breathing slowed down, but the stench seemed to get stronger by the second. Listening carefully, he could just hear voices in the distance over the pounding in his chest. Rick was angrily recounting what happened. Then Joey's voice behind Rick's.

Then Cal's.

"So where is he?"

"How do I know?" Rick snapped back. "He could be halfway up the block by now in somebody's yard. Maybe he ran back to the skating rink."

"No, he couldn't have got that far," Cal responded. The voices got closer, perhaps just around the corner. Mikes stomach clenched itself into a knot, and he was very nearly sick from fear and from hot summer's night garbage.

"That little jerk," he could hear Venetia saying. "First, Sunnie and now him."

"It was your idea to bring them," chided Cal. "But at least Joey is being a man though. Maybe I'll let him in on the stuff. But Mike, man, we may have to leave his tail out here, 'cause time is going." The voices faded again, but the sting of the words hit Mike harder than even the knot in his stomach. A jerk? And all this time he thought Venetia liked him and wanted to be his friend. Now she seemed as mean as Rick. And Joey wouldn't even listen to him. A new knot came up, but this one was in his throat. But then he heard Venetia's voice again, and this time she seemed to be alone.

"Mike?"

He peeked up in time to see her walk just past the alley and head slowly up the street.

"Mike," she called out, now returning to her usual singsong voice.

"Come on; don't be scared. I won't let Rick hit you, I promise. We still need your help tonight, and we're gonna have lots of fun. And Okay," she added "I'm sorry I called you a jerk; I didn't mean it. Just come out, Okay? Nobody's mad; so come on out. Pleeeese?"

Mike was still crouched down between the bags on his hands and knees. His palms were sweating, his knees were sore against the hard asphalt, and his back was starting to hurt. His heart was still pounding and his stomach still felt sick. Maybe she did still like him. She said she was sorry. If he just stood up, this whole thing would be over with, and they could all be friends again. But just then, it suddenly occurred to Mike… to pray. "Dear God," he said inside himself after a moment or so. "What should I do? Please help me." Another half a minute went by. He could still hear Venetia's voice, now distant again. Mike started to push himself from between the bags. But then a strange thing happened. Mike heard something inside his head. A voice that sounded just like his own answered him. "No," he heard himself saying silently. She lied to Pastor Dave about Sunnie. What's to say she's not lying now? Mike was almost startled, but he suddenly felt a resolve, growing bigger and bigger in his chest. He sat back on his heels. That's it, he said to himself. Dad's right. I'm not going with them; and if they're not my friends any more, then they're just not. He was just about to stand, but he tripped and fell back into the heap just as Venetia ran back past the alley. She spoke to someone on the corner.

"He's not here; he would have come out if he was. I know it."

"Alright, get in," said another voice and a car door slammed.

"What's that back there?" someone else asked.

"Oh, that?" he heard Cal reply. "That's just all the garbage from the stores. Let's get out of here."

"Wait!" Mike yelled, but he was drowned out by the sound of engines revving up. By the time he straightened up and picked his way out to the alley entrance, everyone was gone.

Mike's Dilemma

Chapter 19

Mike's Dilemma

Mike looked at his watch. It was just past nine o'clock. He looked up and down the dimly lit street, and it was entirely deserted. The summer night chirping of insects and the low electronic hum of the street light overhead were all he could hear now except, of course, the pounding that started up in his chest again. Before, he was afraid of getting beat up by Rick. Now, he was just plain scared. "Oh, God," he prayed again, "what should I do?" Mike looked around the corner at the florescent circle of light that came out of the store. Should he try to walk back to the skating rink? He looked across the stores in the direction they came from. He was so absorbed in his thoughts on the way that he didn't really look to see the way they came. It was Rick's short cut through several empty lots and around corners. And now that it was dark, he had absolutely no idea how to get back. He didn't carry a phone – his dad said not until he was a teenager. Mike went near the store entrance and peeked in; but he couldn't see anybody behind the counter, and there were no payphones.

Suddenly, a black car pulled up and two men got out and went into the store. Mike saw that they waited; and when someone came out, they engaged him in conversation. Uncertain whether to wait for them to finish or to try to walk someplace, Mike sighed and leaned against the building. "I tried to do the right thing," he said half to himself and half to God, "and now I'm stuck out here at night, alone and lost. And I deserve it too. I never should have left the skating party. I knew it was wrong even before I left, and I went anyway." Mike never felt so scared or sorry about anything in his life. Mike felt the tight lump in his throat again, and a hot tear welled up from his eye and rolled down his cheek. But then, he thought again about Sunday, and what Pastor Dave said during his sermon. *"God is my refuge and my strength. A very present help in trouble."*

Mike stopped crying and looked up. In the distance, he could see the street sign, Hathaway Ave. Mike knew that both his house and the skating rink were not too far from Hathaway, but at night in an unfamiliar part of town, he wasn't sure which one was in which direction. So Mike said another quick prayer, asking God to help him, shoved his hands into his pockets, and started walking. And walking and walking. Thanks to streetlights, it wasn't totally dark, but other than an occasional passing car, the streets of the old mostly unused downtown area were deserted. Only a few scraggly trees, vacant lots and empty warehouses were there to keep him company, along with shadows that threatened to engulf him.

Then to make matters worse, it started to rain. Not heavily, just enough to make the street slick, and Mike uncomfortable as his favorite shirt stuck to his back from the rain and his own nervous perspiration. Mike put his head down, hunched his shoulders against the rain and kept walking. A massive shadow ahead made him look up. With a sickening feeling he recognized the highway overpass high above and realized that he was actually walking *away* from the skating rink all that time - which was over a half an hour. Now chilly and wet, Mike stood under the overpass and wondered what to do now. "It's too far to go back. I know this street…" Mike wracked his brain. He was still on the avenue. "Coming from near my house," he said outloud, Hathaway makes two big turns, and then… wait a minute!"

Suddenly Mike's spirits lifted, and he started to run in the same direction that he was walking. He half-ran, half-walked for another fifteen minutes and soon saw that his hunch was right. Away from downtown meant towards his neighborhood. "All I have to do is turn down Mulberry Street, past the church, then a few more blocks and I'll be home." Mike said to himself. But his stomach tightened up again when he realized that to get home from this direction, he would have to pass the Palmer Mansion. Mike tuned the corner and headed cautiously down Mulberry. Too exhausted now to keep running, he walked as fast as he could and tried not to look at the back of the huge old house as he passed.

"When I get home," he said, distracting himself, "I'll just tell Dad I left the rink early." Mike was trying to think how he could explain how and why he came home alone when his thoughts were interrupted by the sounds of chanting in the distance. He almost forced himself to ignore it and start running again, but then he heard another noise - someone crying - and it was a familiar voice. He crept up across the lawn towards the house and slipped around the side wall, his sneakers crunching in the fresh cedar chips placed during the renovation of the house and yard. He was shocked to see Joey huddled under a bush sobbing.

"Joey? What happened?"

"He punched me in my face!" Joey hissed, wiping his eyes with the heel of his hand and looking up. Mike could see the black eye to prove it. Joey didn't say who hit him, but Mike was sure it had been Rick. Before he could ask, Joey went on.

"You were right about them. They said they were coming out here to some kind of ritual, and I wanted us to come cause it would be fun. But when Venetia and those other kids went out back to make their circle, Cal and Rick made me come with them. They sneaked up to the house and broke the basement window. They said they wanted to get some of the stuff I told them was in the basement. I said I didn't come here to steal nothin' and I was gonna tell. That's when Rick punched me. Cal tried to grab me by my jacket, but I ran."

"Joey," pleaded Mike "Let's go. NOW! We can go to my house, my dad's…"

"But I gotta get my jacket" wailed Joey.

"Forget the stupid jacket - we gotta…"

"My dad's cell phone is in the pocket! It's brand new, and he doesn't know that I have it!" Before Mike could say another word, Joey jumped up and ran towards the back of the house. He stopped short, just at the end of the wall. Mike slid up behind him and they peered around the edge. In the distance under some trees about forty yards away, the group was still moving around in a large circle, maybe fifteen people altogether. Mike couldn't make out what they were saying, but he could make out several of them jumping, twirling and dancing in the dim glow of the solar powered ground lights that had been planted throughout the property. Mike looked in the direction that Joey was now pointing. He could see something dark and crumpled up on the ground under a nearby tree. Hunching down close to the ground, they scurried across. Joey picked up his jacket, put it on, and checked the pockets for the phone.

"It's still here," he said. Looking out from behind the tree, they could see the fence and beyond it the flat doors that they themselves had used to enter the basement. Mike knew that those doors now had a new chain and padlock. Nearby, however, along the base of the house, they could see the gaping hole where the glass was kicked out of the basement window." Mike felt the sickening tightening in his stomach again. "Let's go," he whispered to Joey. They were just about to run when Cal's head appeared at the window. It disappeared again for a second, then he was there again, first pushing out one small box and then another. Then Mike saw several pieces of something shiny and recognized the old suit of armor being pushed out the window piece by piece. Cal then hauled himself back out the window, the now glassless frame just big enough to get through. The boys stood frozen in silence behind the tree. Cal picked up the stuff and started sprinting away from them. Way across beyond the opposite side of the house, Mike could just make out the form of the big black SUV parked at the edge of the road. They waited a few seconds as Cal got smaller in the distance.

"NOW," whispered Mike urgently. When we get to my house, I'll tell my dad to call the …" Suddenly, Mike was cut off in mid-sentence, as a hand grabbed each of them by the neck and pushed them roughly back up against the tree.

"That's what you think, Punk," Rick spat. Joey immediately yelled. Mike almost got away, but Rick was amazingly quick, despite his bulk, and swiftly had Mike's arm in a vise-like grip. Joey wrenched free and ran right into Cal, who heard the noise and rushed back. Cal looked at Mike and snorted.

"I thought we lost you at the 24 hour store."

"Yeah," said Rick, "but now they both saw you take the stuff, and they're talking about calling the police." Cal's lip turned up into a cruel sneer, made all the more menacing by the dim white lights and the night shadows.

"Joey, go get in the car," he said, shoving Joey in the direction of the SUV.

"No! We wanna go home."

"Listen Moron," shot back Cal. "I already told you - all I gotta do is say one word to my father, and your old man is history at McKay Industries and …" Mike cut him off by trying again to yank himself free of Rick.

"LET ME …" but Mike barely got the words out when he saw the silver flash of the knife edge that was suddenly visible in Rick's hand. "You think I'm scared to use this? Huh? HUH?" he said waving it alternately at Joey and Mike. Again, Mike felt cold fingers crawling up his back, and he was almost too stunned to move.

"Hey, put that thing away," said Cal. Rick did with a snicker, but Joey meekly walked over across and climbed into the SUV. Mike didn't resist, as Rick pulled him by the arm and shoved him into the back seat next to Joey. He then climbed in himself but left the door open. Suddenly, Venetia appeared and ran up to Cal, who was still standing there.

"Is everything OK? We heard yelling in the distance, and you guys didn't come back to the circle."

"We gotta leave. Go tell everybody it's time to get outta here "

"Why? We're not done and …"

"Cause the police are coming, OK?" said Cal, with a new edge to his voice. "So shut up and do what I tell you! And move it!" Venetia looked shocked and angry, but she left and returned in less than five minutes. Cal was already revving the engine as she climbed into the front seat and strapped on the seat belt. She turned when she heard Rick slam the door closed.

"What on earth - Mike! How did you get back here, and what's all that stuff in the back?"

"Didn't I just tell you to shut up?" snapped Cal. Then he pushed the accelerator to the floor, and the five of them screeched off .

* * * * * *

Shamael saw everything from the moment Mike's mom dropped him off at the rink. He knew Mike well enough to tell that he was really sorry for what he had done, and as soon as Mike was truly sorry, Shamael knew that the Holy One, as always, forgave. But now, his concern was growing as he and Jediael floated together silently watching the SUV careen through the slick dark streets of Chesterton, speeding and swerving dangerously close to the road's edge. Presently, Hanniel joined them.

"What are you two doing out here?" he asked.

"Watching out, just like you," answered Shamael. Where is your Danny?

"Not far. Their grandmother, Mrs. Gains, just picked the boys up from the rink. Barachel is with them. The three friends watched the tiny red car thread carefully through the streets with their silvery companion floating above, while the black SUV swerved around another corner a few blocks ahead.

"Guess there's no stopping this," Jediael added, nodding towards the SUV.

"No" replied Shamael. "My Mike had been having a little struggle with himself over this whole affair, but by the time he said no and tried to talk Joey out of it, things had gone too far."

"And my Joey," added Jediael, "was just determined to impress Cal and Rick, no matter what they wanted him to do."

"But didn't Joey know better?" asked Barachel, who had just come up. "He was there when Pastor Dave spoke to all of them the first time."

"I'm sure he knows better now," said Jediael with a note of sadness in his voice. "I was so hoping that Mike would have convinced Joey not to go, but now look at the mess they're both in."

"Listen," said Hanniel, "it's a good thing we can converse faster than humans move because that SUV is heading for a disaster. What are we going to do?"

"We have to do something" said Jediael. "We can't just let him - let them…"

Suddenly, the angels saw a bright flash of light; and in less than an instant, Magdiel once again appeared before them. He stood silently with his back towards the SUV, and his right hand held up as if to say "Stop."

"But if there is an accident…" began Jediael.

"They will not all die," said Magdiel softly.

"Won't they all be badly hurt?" asked Shamael.

"Has it not been prayed that these children would come to see their need for the Holy One? Has it not also been prayed that they would forsake pride and fear to help one another? Do not worry. In time it will all work together for good."

"For those who love God and submit to Him," replied Jediael. "We know."

"Are we allowed to intervene at all?" asked Hanniel.

"Yes," said Magdiel. And he disappeared as suddenly as he arrived. The four angels looked up to see the SUV speeding towards the sharp Hathaway Avenue curve. Mrs. Gains' car was about two blocks away, cautiously approaching.

Mike's Dilemma

"The will of the Holy One must be done" said Jediael quietly, "but will any of those kids even know what to do?"

"Let's give them some help," said Shamael.

"What kind of help?" asked the others.

"The tangible kind," he replied. " 'Entertaining angels unaware' kind of help."

Jannette Morrow

Chapter 15

Mike's Dilemma

Mike wasn't sure what he wanted to do more - cover his mouth to keep from throwing up or cover his eyes to keep from seeing what was going on. Rick was hooting at the top of his lungs and the SUV lurched with another sickening skid of the tires against the wet asphalt. Cal had sped off before anyone in the back seat thought about putting on a seatbelt. With every left turn, Mike slammed into Joey, who banged into Rick who would shove him back. Another right turn and Mike pressed into the door with Joey sliding into him. Only Venetia was belted into the front passenger seat, but that didn't stop her yells and cries, barely audible over the wailing guitar, banging drums, and driving bass that were screaming through the SUV's high performance audio system. Mike wondered if the smell of burning rubber was real or just his imagination. Suddenly pressed against the seat back as Cal raced down another street, Mike had the presence of mind to try to put on his safety belt; and as he was just ready to click it, he noticed that his door was unlocked. Suddenly, Mike had an idea. Could they? Did he dare? He let the seat belt snap back and turned towards Joey, but Cal suddenly slammed the brakes, slapping him into the back of the driver's seat and pitching Joey forward. Mike wound up on his knees on the floor when the wheels spun again, and the car shot off and swung a wide curve, pitching Mike forward almost on his face. He managed to reach up and grab Joey by his arm, pulling his ear down towards him.

"Switch seats with me, and hold onto your phone," Mike rasped in a horse whisper. Joey, of course, barely heard him over the din. By now, Cal was racing down Hathaway Avenue. He and Rick were loudly chanting the words to the song with the voice on the tape, curse words included, and passing a can of beer between them.

"What?" whispered back Joey. "How're we gonna call anybody?"

"Just make sure you got it," returned Mike, still on his knees. Joey felt for the phone while he scrambled past Mike, next to the door. Cal was taking another swig of beer and didn't even seem to notice. Mike stayed crouched down, turned, and leaning over Joey's lap, gripped the door handle. A few seconds passed, and Mike felt the deceleration he was waiting for.

"WHAT'RE YOU…" cried Joey, but he didn't finish his sentence because Mike yanked the handle and shoved Joey's hips with all his might.

"JUMP!" Mike barely had time to see Joey roll away from the SUV when Cal hit the gas again sending a wail of screeching tires into the air. At the same time, Rick, who saw the door open, swore loudly and made a move to grab Mike, but the SUV suddenly lurched and then veered, almost as if it were moving sideways. Without thinking, Mike dove out of the still open door. The world whirled around him, and he felt as if he fell into a vacuum. Then…nothing.

* * * * * *

"You mean…? Why it's been centuries since I've done anything like that. What about you?" asked Jediael

"Never," said Shamael. But I know many who have. How about you Hanniel?

"Me? Oh, I spent some time as a hobo not too long ago, before my Danny was born. I used to shake my cup right outside of a church. You'd be amazed at the number of Christians who passed me by without even a word," said Hanniel with a grin.

"Oh, go on!" said Jediael.

"Gladly. There was one lady who I saw every week. Never parted with a red cent but she sure gave me a piece of her mind. Called me a vagabond and a loiterer, she did. You just wait till I see her in Heaven."

"She's going to Heaven?" asked Jediael.

"Of course, she is," laughed Hanniel. "And I plan to tease her for ten thousand years…"

"Will you two get serious?" said Shamael because just then, the SUV was airborne with doors open and heading for a clump of small trees.

"I am serious," Hanniel replied, but if we're going to do it, we'll need permission from the very top."

"You all go then," said Barachel. "I'll stay by the car with my Teddy, Danny and Mother Gains."

When the three angels stepped out of time into eternity in Heaven, time of course didn't stop. But it was as though the SUV hung in mid-air with Mike and Joey frozen where they were. The three angels instantly entered the presence of God himself.

For a moment, they didn't even want to go back. Music, light, peace, and beauty were everywhere. There was wonderful singing and cries of "Holy, Holy, Holy" filled the air. A cherub appeared and turned one of his four faces towards the trio.

"You are seeking permission?" he asked.

"Yes," they answered.

"Wait here." He flew towards the throne, then the mighty Voice rolled towards them.

"Advance." The three stepped forward.

"You have My permission. Proceed." They bowed their thanks.

* * * * * *

Mike felt himself lying flat on his back in the damp stubble even before he opened his eyes. He blinked at the dark sky and his eyes began to focus. The quiet all around seemed deathly. When his vision cleared, he noticed two faces looking down at him. Joey's and Danny's too, of all people. But there was an unfamiliar face, a grownup. He was an Indian-looking fellow, tall handsome, and had on the cleanest pair of jeans that Mike had ever seen on a guy. Instinctively, Mike reached up his hand, and the tall guy pulled him up into a sitting position.

"That was a pretty amazing flight you took." the man said with a grin. Mike, still a bit dazed, looked around. Several yards up and to his left, he could see the edge of the road. The ground leveled a bit where he was sitting but pitched downward again on his right.

"Are you OK?" said Joey, looking worried. "After you pushed me out, I started running, but I saw a car coming, and it was Danny and his grandma. I skinned my knee and tore my pants, but I wasn't hurt."

"Yeah," added Danny who was holding a flashlight. "She took the cell phone to call for help." Mike looked towards where Danny was pointing and could make out the tiny red car parked by the road side and an older dark-skinned woman with white hair peering down at them, cell phone to her ear.

"My friends and I saw you from beyond the trees down there," said the stranger, pointing down the embankment. "You looked like you could use some help. Looks to me like you're in pretty good shape, considering. Any pain anywhere?" Mike reached and felt his own shoulders, knees, and legs. He was sore and had a few bruises on his arms and legs, but amazingly he wasn't really hurt either. Before he thought about it, he stood up without any help. "Well, praise the Lord," said Blue Jeans with a chuckle. "But maybe we'd better check on your other friends. He nodded and waved towards Danny's grandma, Mrs. Gains, then turned and started the rest of the way down the embankment.

Mike, Joey, and Danny picked their way down behind him. Following the beam of the flashlight through the stand of now smashed young trees, they came to a huge oak, which towered over an awful sight. The battered SUV lay on its side, the front smashed in by the massive trunk of the old tree. The stench of burning rubber was in the air and debris lay scattered around, barely visible in the foggy darkness. The beam of light fell on something shiny. Mike moved to look at it more closely; it looked like the head piece from the suit of armor that Cal had taken out of the Palmer mansion and packed into the SUV. As his eyes adjusted to the darkness, he noted that more of the muddy debris was looking familiar: baseball cards, an old lamp, Joey's skates.

But then they heard someone crying from inside the SUV. The passenger side was up, and Mike took the flashlight. He and Joey got as close as they could to the car and shined the light into the open window. Mike saw an elbow and forearm clinging to the side. Venetia's head appeared. And Mike recoiled in spite of himself to see Venetia's usually pretty face so altered. She was crying, but her tears could barely flow past the bruises and swelling caused by the airbag when it deployed. She was trying to say something, but Mike could barely understand her past her bloody and swollen lips. She started to wheeze something that sounded like, "I didn't know…", but a sharp yell from Danny interrupted from a clump of bushes nearby. Mike ran over to join him. To his horror, there was Rick dimly illuminated by a distant street lamp above, sprawled out on the ground. He'd apparently been thrown from the SUV during its flight over the road edge. His head was bloody, and there was a big bleeding gash in one leg. The other leg was bent in a weird angle - clearly broken.

"Look!" gasped Danny. " What are we gonna do? What if he's dead?" For a few seconds, Mike could only stare speechless at the awful sight. Then he knelt down and put his cheek near Rick's nose and two fingers on his neck just under his jaw. Mike wasn't sure exactly what he was supposed to feel, but he remembered seeing a picture in one of his mom's nursing textbooks. He could barely feel Rick's breath on his cheek, but there was something, and he felt a fast pulse in his neck.

"He's not dead," Blue Jeans called over from the SUV where he was helping Venetia to get out.

"I wonder if Grandma got anybody on the phone," said Danny. But before he could turn to run back up, they saw two more guys walking towards them from behind the old oak. There was a black guy, who was wearing a polo shirt, and he was as handsome and clean cut as Blue Jeans. The third was a big guy wearing cut-off jeans and sneakers and a long blond ponytail. He had on a tee shirt that said 'Radical for Christ'. Radical went over to help Blue Jeans with Venetia. Polo Shirt walked over and knelt beside Rick, and Joey followed him over. Mike wandered around to the other side of the car, where the roof stood perpendicular to the ground.

"Here's Venetia, and Rick is over there," he said. "But where's Cal?" Mike looked down the SUV roof to the ground. In the dim light he could barely make out the edge of a white sock and the tread of a sneaker bottom. Neither was moving. Just as the awful truth began to dawn on him, Blue Jeans came over and laid a hand on his arm.

"Cal," Mike said, his voice suddenly shaking, "is he … is he…" Blue Jeans looked at Mike steadily for a moment, and then he slowly nodded.

But his gaze was so warm and friendly that Mike suddenly felt comforted. Just then, Radical set Venetia on the ground a few feet away from Rick. He stood up and put a beefy arm around Danny's shoulder.

"Danny, you run back up the embankment as fast as you can," he said. "The paramedics are on their way, so tell Mother Gains to walk back to the turn and tell them to come down to the old oak. Then come right back."

"Right," said Danny, and he sped off. Blue Jeans put his arm around Mike's shoulder and led him away from the SUV towards the others. "Now, if you'll let me hold that big hankie in your pocket, I think we can make a bandage until help comes," he said. Mike almost got a chance to wonder how on earth this guy knew about the handkerchief that his mom had tucked into his pants pocket, but things were happening too fast. By now, Radical had an arm around Venetia, and she had stopped crying, but Rick started to moan.

"Is she gonna be OK?" said Mike, as he gave Blue Jeans the handkerchief. "Don't worry," said Radical with a chuckle. "Believe it or not, she is." Blue Jeans quickly folded up the handkerchief, stepped over to the bushes, and stooped down opposite Polo Shirt to place it against the bleeding wound on Rick's leg. Polo Shirt placed his palm on it and pressed down hard into the wound. Mike suddenly felt sad. Cal and Rick had been awfully mean to them, but seeing them like this made Mike feel sorrier for them than anything else. In fact, he might have burst into tears were it not for Blue

Jean's gentle pat on his shoulder.

"Why don't you kneel down and help them while I go check on the ambulance," he said. Mike hesitated, but Radical gave him a warm grin. "Go on," he said "You can do it. We're here with you, and so is He," he said pointing to the Name on his tee shirt. Blue Jeans gave Mike's shoulders a reassuring squeeze and then walked towards the foot of the embankment.

"Untie your windbreaker," Polo Shirt said to Venetia. She untied the jacket from around her waist and handed it Joey who put it over Rick at Polo Shirt's instruction and added his own jacket too. Polo Shirt motioned for Mike to start pressing on the wound. Suddenly, Rick began to come around even more, and he opened his mouth as though he would cry out. Polo Shirt reached over, put a hand on each side of Rick's head, and looked him in the eye.

"HUSH!" he said. Mike wasn't sure if he was comforting Rick or scolding him, but either way Rick shut up - quick. Mike kept pressing the leg wound as hard as he could all the while looking from Radical to Polo Shirt and then over at Blue Jeans in the dim light of the street lamps that lined the streets above them. There was something eerily familiar about these guys, but Mike couldn't put his finger on it. "They act like they know us" he said to himself. "Where do we know them from?" Mike looked at Radical again and tried to remember if he'd ever seen him in church. Radical looked back at him, smiled, and winked. All of a sudden, Blue Jeans spoke.

"Here they come," he called back to them.

Immediately afterwards, they heard sirens wailing and the shouts and footsteps of a crowd running toward them from the road. The next few minutes went by like a blur. Paramedics and emergency medical personnel were leaping down the embankment with several policemen right behind them. Danny was scrambling down after them, and Mike could see Mrs. Gains and a now awake Teddy carefully picking their way down. Police and paramedics were shouting questions, which Mike, Danny, Joey and even Venetia answered the best they could. A needle, then a bag of fluid being attached to Rick's arm, and a face mask for oxygen were put over his nose and mouth. Another group had gathered around Venetia, and she was being lifted onto a stretcher. Even Mike and Joey were being strapped into special chairs and carried up to a waiting ambulance over their protests that they were alright.

"You two were in the car," said Mother Gains. You'd better go just in case. Besides, your moms will be waiting for you at the hospital." More police, and now a fire truck. Someone crawled into the open door of the SUV and came out quickly, shaking his head. All the time, red and white lights flashed in continuous circles. One ambulance pulled off, and a police officer was walking beside them as they were being carried up. Mike looked up and realized that he recognized him from church. Mother Gains and Teddy were following.

"You guys were great," Officer Thompson said. "You did exactly the right things."

"Well," admitted Mike, "we had help. There were these three guys who came from the other side and…hey, where are they?" Both boys looked around. People were still down the embankment and gathered around the SUV but the three guys were gone - no Radical, no Polo shirt, and no Blue Jeans.

"Are you sure?" asked Officer Thompson, after hearing the boy's description. "I don't recall seeing anyone like that down there." They climbed up to Hathaway Avenue just in time to see a paramedic close the doors to Rick's ambulance. Mike asked him if he saw a tall guy with straight black hair and jeans or a guy in a polo shirt standing by Rick.

"No," he replied before climbing in and driving away, sirens screaming.

"But they helped take care of us," protested Mike to the paramedic who was securing him and Joey in their ambulance. "They came from behind the big tree down there."

"Kid, I didn't see anybody fitting those descriptions down there," returned the paramedic. He walked around to the driver's side of the ambulance and opened the door and climbed in.

"Besides," said his partner just before sitting down, "there's nothing beyond that old oak but a barrier and a sixty foot drop-off to the highway below. If anybody came from that direction, he would have had to fly."

Mike's Dilemma

Chapter 16

Mike's Dilemma

So it seemed that no one saw the three guys except Mike, Danny, Joey, Rick, and Venetia. And Mother Gains too, but only from a distance. Mike and Joey described the whole thing to her as they waited in the emergency room.

"It was surely the angels of the Lord that helped you all down there. But my heart is troubled about that McKay boy - and for his people." She only shook her head and didn't say anything else until Ms. Meg and Ms. Ellen came and found them. Mike's dad was there too, he brought Joey's mom and dad with him in his car.

"Did you all hear about Cal McKay?" they asked.

"Believe me," Mother Gains sighed, "we know all about it, and I'll let Mike and Joey tell you the whole story."

Both boys were discharged early Saturday morning with a clean bill of health after a night of "observation" in the emergency room. They heard that Venetia would probably go home that afternoon, but Rick would be laid up for weeks. And tell his dad the whole thing is exactly what Mike did. Meg wanted him to get into bed and rest some more, but he was still too worked up to sleep, despite the fact that he was still exhausted. So Mike Sr. poured some breakfast cereal and milk and listened to his son tell the whole tale from the beginning, starting with the conversation that he and Joey had with Cal and Venetia at the burger place and ending with everything that happened that night. When Mike finished his story, he sat staring into his untouched glass of milk. Mike Sr. let the silence hang there a few moments, sensing that his son wasn't quite finished. The grandfather clock in the living room chimed a distant eight a.m.

"Dad," said Mike, now wiping a stray tear with the back of his hand. "It's like it's all my fault. I should have told on them. If I said something, maybe nobody would have gotten hurt." Mike Sr. rested his chin in his hand and looked at his son.

"Mike, while it's certainly true that you should have said something, what happened to Cal and Rick is certainly not all your fault. And only God knows whether such a tragedy would have still happened, even if you did tell." He reached across the table and took both Mike's hands in his big ones. "But God has been mighty good to you boys and Venetia too, by bringing you out safe. Let's say we pray right now and thank him for that."

After praying with his dad and napping the rest of the morning, Mike got dressed and wandered back over to the Palmer house. After all, it was Saturday, and Mike kind of wanted to talk to the young pastor. So he sat in the chair that was offered to him and again told the whole story from beginning to end. Pastor Dave didn't say much at first, not even when Mike got to the part about the three kind strangers who helped them and then apparently disappeared. He only chuckled and told Mike to look up in his Bible Hebrews 13th chapter and second verse. But then his voice got serious.

"Mike, I can tell something is bothering you. What is it?"

"Pastor Dave," said Mike, "do you think it's my fault? I mean, if I had said no instead of saying I would help them, maybe Rick wouldn't have gotten hurt and maybe Cal wouldn't have died?"

"Mike" replied Pastor Dave, "yes, it's very true that you should have said something earlier. And who knows? Had you told your mom and dad or even me, maybe this could have been prevented. But it's also possible that had you said no, they would have made the same plans without you and possibly with the same consequences. Only God knows whether or not things would have been different or the same." Mike grinned a bit and looked down at his sneakers.

"That's almost exactly what my dad said." Pastor Dave put his hands on Mike's shoulders and looked him straight in the eye.

"They had already made up their minds to do something they knew was wrong. Wrong actions often bring bad consequences, sometimes even tragic ones. You, Joey, and even Rick and Venetia should be extremely grateful to God, because He has given you all another chance to let Him work in your lives. Do you understand?"

"I think so," said Mike. He was silent a minute but couldn't help asking another question. "What about you? Are you mad at me and Joey? And aren't you mad that they used your yard and broke into your house and stole stuff?" At this, Pastor Dave sat back and looked at Mike thoughtfully.

"No, I'm not mad at you and Joey. I'm sure you thought Cal and Rick would hurt you if you didn't do what they wanted. And I can't deny that I was very angry at first. To be very honest, our whole family is still praying very hard about how or even if we should try to recover our damages for the property and the objects. And I know with God's help, we can forgive. More importantly though," he went on "right now Rick, Venetia, and their families, and especially Cal's family, need all the love and support we can give them. And our prayers that they all come to know Jesus."

"What about Cal?" asked Mike, now getting to the heart of what was really troubling him. "You said that if a person dies without Jesus, they can't go to heaven. Did Cal go to…?" Mike again stopped before saying what his mom always told him was a "bad word." Pastor Dave looked steadily at Mike a few moments and then looked away into the distance.

"Well, I'll tell you something. I was talking on the phone this morning with Pastor Roberts about all of this. He told me that years ago, when Cal was just a bit younger than you are now, he used to come to Sunday school at Community Fellowship. So he heard the gospel, and he knew who Jesus Christ is. Who knows if he didn't ask God to forgive him in those last moments and is right now in God's presence? Only God Himself knows, and I guess we'll have to leave such things to Him."

Chapter 11

Mike's Dilemma

Pastor Dave enlisted the boys to help in the final stages of cleaning up the old mansion, and they were there nearly every day. Pastor Dave's wife April, his mom and dad, as well as several other church members, were all hard at work too. Soon, even the damage from the break-in was so well repaired it was as if it didn't even happen. Finally, on the Friday before Labor Day, Pastor Dave called over Mike, Joey, Danny, and all the rest of the workers and announced that it was time "to let the whole Community Fellowship Church family and the neighborhood know about our plans. Pastor Roberts has given permission for fellowship after church this Sunday to be here at the Palmer House," he added. "It will be a potluck supper and barbecue, and everyone's invited."

That Sunday was altogether a special day. Mike was in church with his mom and dad, and Mr. and Mrs. Edwards were there with Joey. Even Danny and Teddy's mom, Ms. Ellen was there with them, and so was their grandmother, Mother Gains. And this time when the invitation was given, Joey got up and went to the front all on his own without anyone asking or telling him.

When Sunday afternoon came, Mike, his friends and their parents were filling their plates around the buffet table on the freshly mowed lawn behind the old Palmer mansion. Nearly everyone from the church who didn't go away for the holiday weekend had come. People stood around in groups eating and talking, while others relaxed in one of the many folding chairs scattered around the lawn. When the last of the parishioners of Community Fellowship Church had arrived, as well as several guests from the community, Pastor Palmer leaned over and spoke to his dad, Mr. Jack Palmer.

"Well, Pop," he said, "do you want to make the announcement now?"

"Yes," said the old gentleman. As he stood up from his seat and moved to the center of the area, everyone turned in their chairs to face him.

"As many of you know," he began, "our family has been in this community and lived in this very home for over a century. Now that me and the Miss's are getting on a bit in years" (he smiled at old Mrs. Palmer as he spoke), we thought that now would be a good time to leave some sort of legacy to the people of this town that we love so much. About a year ago, we sat down as a family to think of a way that we could use this old house to benefit the people here. So for the past several months and especially this summer, we have been fixing and cleaning towards our goal. The plan..." Mr. Palmer looked at his son who nodded encouragement.

"Well, the plan is three parts. First, we'll be using the west wing of the house as a bread and breakfast. We'll hire all local people, and any profits will be donated to local charities, including Community Fellowship Church. Second, we'll be turning the east wing into a Senior Citizens' center. Like me, lots of folks in this community have been getting older, and many have told me that they would like to have a bigger place to gather, participate in interesting activities, have a meal, and reminisce. Last of all, we'll be opening up the basement and the yard to our local youth. They'll be able to study after school, play ball, and other games. And if they need help with homework or something, well, any of our seniors who would like to help out are more than welcome to come over. Is that about it, son?"

"Yep, Pop, it sure is," answered Pastor Dave with a smile, and everyone applauded. Pastor Dave went on to thank the community board and the local chamber of commerce for all their help with the project. Then he said, "We are especially happy to have Mother Emma Gains and her daughter Ellen Edwards as first guests of our bed and breakfast this Labor Day weekend. Everyone applauded again as old Mr. and Mrs. Palmer, followed by Pastor Dave, his wife April and the rest of the family came and sat where Mike, Danny, Joey, and Teddy were sitting. All the guests had settled back to eating and talking when Ms. Ellen turned to Mrs. Gains.

"Mom, I guess you have been a part of this old place almost as much as the Palmer family," she said.

"Yes, I certainly have," said Mrs. Gains, and her wrinkled face seemed to break up into a hundred smiles as she spoke. "I remember the old times," she said, reaching over to take old Mrs. Palmer's hand. "Mabel, you and me were just girls when we worked for Mr. David Palmer. That was even before you and Jack were married and young David was born."

"You remember my grandfather?" asked Pastor Dave.

"Of course, I do! How could I forget him?" exclaimed Mrs. Gains. No one could ever want to work for a smarter, kinder, or fairer man than

Mike's Dilemma

Mr. David Palmer, Esquire. He was good to everyone - rich, poor, black, white, whatever. And you couldn't say that about everybody, especially back in those days. It was a sad day when he passed on, except I know he went to be with the Lord."

"Yes" chimed in Mrs. Mabel Palmer, still holding Mrs. Gaines's hand and with a far away look in her eyes. "He was right here in the house when it happened." That caused Mike to sit up. Suddenly, he was interested in the grownup's conversation.

"Mr. Palmer," he ventured during the pause in the discussion, "way back then when your father was alive...I mean; is all the stuff they say really true?"

"Stuff - what stuff?" asked Ms. Meg.

"You know" said Joey. "The stuff about a bank robbery, and money in the basement, and murders - all the stuff people around here say happened."

"Oh, THAT stuff," laughed the old man. "Well, I'll tell you," he said, leaning forward and holding up his hands for emphasis. All the kids and grown ups within earshot put down their knives and forks and leaned in to hear what Mr. Jack Palmer had to say. Were the old rumors true or not?

"You see," he said, still laughing, "there are lots of stories about this old place, and truthfully most of them are just rumor. Some, though, are based in fact. Years and years ago, this land and lots of the surrounding area were one big farm. But not too long after the turn of the century when my old pop was just a boy, half of this old place was a boarding house that operated from then, through prohibition, the depression, the big war in the 1940's right up through the mid 1960's. All sorts of folk lived here, including some that were bootleggers.

"Bootleggers? What's that?" asked Danny.

"In prohibition times, around about the 1920's, it was against the law to buy or sell liquor. So some folks bought it illegally, and some made their own. In fact, right up stairs on the third floor was a bathtub full of home-made gin…"

"But what about the people?" Joey asked insistently. "Didn't somebody rob a bank and get murdered or something?"

"Well, son," replied the old man, "there was some truth to that one, only it wasn't a real bank. My pop said that when he was a teenager and prohibition was still on, one of the bootleggers secretly dug a big hole in the basement and stashed his bootlegging cash there. He called it his 'bank.' One night his partners accused him of cheating them. Needless to say, when things came to blows, he ran downstairs for his cash and fell in the hole. Hurt himself kind of bad and had to be carried out. When he didn't come back, folks said his partners killed him. Pop said the cops ended up arresting the lot of them and carried them all off to jail. My grandfather told the police that he didn't know about the stash, and fortunately for him they believed him. He did know about the gin though, and got rid of it before the law caught up with his boarders."

"Then what about the story of the ghost?" asked Mike. "Where did that come from?"

"Oh, that old story?" laughed Mrs. Mabel Palmer. "That one really was just a lot of 'stuff'."

"Yes" put in Mother Gains "I can tell you how that one got started. It all began with Miss Rosa Thompson who ran the boarding house during World War II, when Mr. David Palmer was busy with his law practice. Times were hard, but Miss Rosa managed to keep the doors open.

"That's right," added Mrs. Palmer. Emma and I were just young girls when we would come 'round after school. Sometimes we could make a little extra change cleaning up, changing the beds, and whatnot. That's how I met my Jack," she said, with a smile at old Mr. Palmer. Mother Gains continued.

"One of the workers got to stealing from the pantry. Miss Rosa would have given her the food had she asked, and told her so, even after she was caught. 'Share and share alike,' she said, 'but we can't share all round if folks steal.' Miss Rosa didn't want to let her go, with the war on and all, but when the stealing continued, she didn't have any choice. Mr. Palmer said she had to go. Miss Rosa continued to live here until after the war. Her heart got bad, and she died peacefully in her sleep at the age of eighty-two. But after she died, that same worker started spreading rumors that Miss Rosa's ghost was haunting the Palmer mansion. I guess she was trying to keep folks from coming. It didn't harm business none, but the rumor held on, even long after the boarding house was closed."

"Well," said Mrs. Perkins, "I guess that puts an end to all that old talk!" And everybody listening agreed.

Sunday afternoon edged on towards evening, but the fun continued. There were barbecued spareribs, then hot dogs and hamburgers and more potato salad and corn on the cob than they all could eat. Each family brought their own special dish, and Mike tasted everything he could from beans and rice to sushi. Danny actually won a game of horseshoes, and Teddy finally got the ball over the net during the volleyball game. Neither Mike nor Joey couldn remember the last time they had so much fun, though Joey was a little disappointed that there really wasn't a ghost in the Palmer house. He soon forgot it though, when Sunnie mustered up the courage (at Mike's prompting) to tell him she really liked him and if he wanted to 'go to a movie together sometime'. Not only did he say "yes," but it was the first time since being best friends, that Mike ever saw Joey blush.

Finally, the evening drew to a close and everyone pitched in to help clean up, stack chairs and bring the leftover food into the house, and Mike, Joey, Danny, and even Teddy helped to the very end. When they were ready to leave, Pastor Dave came down to walk them to the gate.

"Pastor Dave," said Mike, "you told me to look up Hebrews 13:2. Do you really think that those three guys who helped us were real angels?"

"The word 'angel' means <u>messenger</u> replied Pastor Dave. "Whoever they were, they were certainly sent by God to show you all what to do when you needed help."

"But don't forget, Pastor," said Mike, Sr. "no one but the kids and Mother Gains saw them, and nobody saw them leave."

"True," said Pastor Dave, laughing. "And some folks may think I'm crazy, but, yes, I think you boys really did see your guardian angels. Maybe you didn't 'entertain' them the way the writer of Hebrews was talking about, but I'm sure they enjoyed your company!"

By now, they were all well passed the gate so Pastor Dave gave them a final wave and Mike, his friends, and family continued on their way home with Mike and Joey walking ahead.

"So," said Mike. "What made you finally join the church?" Joey had to admit that it was Teddy of all people that convinced him. "He was reading his kiddy Bible, when he looked up and said, 'Since Jesus saved your life, you should accept him into your heart.' He was right, I guess, so I did."

"What about me?" laughed Danny, pushing Joey's head from behind. "I told you first, remember?"

"Yeah," Joey said, grinning and giving him a friendly shove back. "You did."

Epilogue

Mike's Dilemma

"That must have been some fight," smiled Shamael to the others, as they floated invisibly in the night air above the group.

"You better believe it" returned Barachel laughing. Awmal and Nawgaf gave it all they had but Jediael and I showed them a thing or two."

"So all things did work together for good for our boys," observed Hanniel. "And now that they know Christ, maybe they can help Rick and Venetia to know him too." Jediael didn't say much more about the battle; he didn't have to. They all knew how viciously Awmal, Nawgaf, and all the demons could fight when they were about to lose someone to the Kingdom of God. But it did make the angels rejoice all the more. And Hanniel and Shamael couldn't help but notice that Jediael seemed to be smiling more than he had in the last three hundred years or so.

Mike's mind was a-whirl with the idea of guardian angels, demons, and the fight of good against evil. Mike looked up at the twinkling stars. "Could it be?" he thought. "Did we really meet our guardian angels?"

Mike didn't know it, but if he could have seen into the unseen world, he would have found himself looking directly up into Shamael's smiling face, as he stood above and before them. He could have smiled on at Mike for hours, but he was interrupted.

"I told you my Danny would be the first one to do things right," called Hanniel from where he and Barrachel were watching, as Danny and

Teddy climbed into bed.

"What about my Teddy?" returned Barrachel. "He was pretty sharp too, you know." But Shamael just went back to smiling, and Jediael had to smile with him. All four angels knew that not only did Mike finally make the right decision, but that and he Joey were now Christians because of the Holy One. He deserved all the credit, even if he did use Danny and Teddy and everyone else to help.

"Our guys will be teenagers soon," said Shamael thoughtfully, "and we'll have other children to look after. Do you think they'll be ready? After all, Awmal, Nawgaf and the rest are still out there."

"Oh I think so," replied Jediael. "And the Holy One will always send angels to protect his own, whether it's us or others. By the way, Hanniel, you never told us what you did with the money."

"You mean from the other time I was in human form?" Hanniel said laughing. "I gave it to a real hobo, of course!"

Jannette Morrow

Main Street Publishing, Inc.
206 E. Main Street Suite 207
P.O.Box 696
Jackson, Tn 38301

Toll Free #: 866-457-7379
or
Local #: 731-427-7379

Visit us on the web:
www.mainstreetpublishing.com
www.mspbooks.com

E-Mail: mspsupport@charterinternet.com